Coastal Corpse

A MANGO BAY MYSTERY

COASTAL CORPSE

MARTY AMBROSE

FIVE STAR
A part of Gale, Cengage Learning

GALE
CENGAGE Learning

Farmington Hills, Mich • San Francisco • New York • Waterville, Maine
Meriden, Conn • Mason, Ohio • Chicago

Five Star™ Publishing, a part of Cengage Learning, Inc.

LIBRARY OF CONGRESS CATALOGING-IN-PUBLICATION DATA

Names: Ambrose, Marty, author.
Title: Coastal corpse : a Mango Bay mystery / Marty Ambrose.
Description: First Edition. | Waterville, Maine : Five Star a part of Cengage Learning, Inc. 2016.
Identifiers: LCCN 2016001561 (print) | LCCN 2016006278 (ebook) | ISBN 9781432832018 (hardback) | ISBN 1432832018 (hardcover) | ISBN 9781432831950 (ebook) | ISBN 143283195X (ebook)
Subjects: LCSH: Women journalists—Fiction. | Murder—Investigation—Fiction. | Florida—Fiction. | BISAC: FICTION / Mystery & Detective / Women Sleuths. | FICTION / Mystery & Detective / General. | GSAFD: Mystery fiction.
Classification: LCC PS3601.M368 C63 2016 (print) | LCC PS3601.M368 (ebook) | DDC 813/.6—dc23
LC record available at http://lccn.loc.gov/2016001561

First Edition. First Printing: July 2016
Find us on Facebook– https://www.facebook.com/FiveStarCengage
Visit our website– http://www.gale.cengage.com/fivestar/
Contact Five Star™ Publishing at FiveStar@cengage.com

Printed in the United States of America
1 2 3 4 5 6 7 20 19 18 17 16

ACKNOWLEDGMENTS

I would like to thank my family, as always, for being my best buddies and best critics—especially my husband, Jim (the uber-journalist), and my mom. They are always there in my corner with suggestions and editing advice.

Also, I have to thank my agent and friend, Roberta Brown. She is the best of the best as my business partner and friend. My success is her success!

Lastly, I would like to express my appreciation to Tiffany Schofield and all of the splendid people at Five Star for letting the Mallie adventures continue.

Chapter One

"It's official: this island is dead," I announced, breezing into the shabby-but-not-so-chic *Coral Island Observer* newsroom, my fringed hobo bag swinging behind me. "And I'm ready to die—of boredom."

So I was being a little dramatic.

Okay, maybe a lot.

Glancing around the deserted office with its semi-decrepit furniture and recently installed indoor/outdoor carpeting (pea green, no less), no one was there to respond. Only graveyard-like silence answered me—and the smell of onions from the hoagie I'd scarfed down for lunch yesterday.

No Sandy the Secretary. No Anita the Editor.

Sigh.

Not that I expected our secretary-cum-receptionist-cum everything, Sandy, to be at her desk. She had gotten married two weeks ago to her fiancé, Jimmy, and they were still off on their honeymoon in St. Augustine. I was happy for them—truly. But I missed my office buddy with her chirpy, upbeat personality and constant stream of "diet of the month" talk.

I *had* expected Anita to be here this morning—if only to hammer at me about my latest story. But her cubicle sat empty, too. Guess I lucked out on that one—for now.

My cell phone beeped with Sandy's latest text message: *Love the B & B. Heading out for a carriage ride through Old Town. Then the "Ghost Walk" tonite.* I smiled. How fitting, since Jimmy's mother—Madame Geri—touted herself as Coral Island's freelance psychic.

I stared at the message. Their connubial bliss just made *my* situation seem all the more confusing—and weird, now that I was *engaged.*

I gulped as the last word echoed through my mind like a rolling wave, not sure whether to eagerly dip my toes in the water or run for the sea oats.

Is that what awaited me? Marital bliss like Sandy and Jimmy's for the rest of my life? Or one of those marriages Lord Byron described with biting wit as "wishing each other not divorced, but dead"? Unfortunately, being a comparative literature major, I was steeped in every bad bookish take on marriage from Anna Karenina to Madame Bovary. Maybe I needed to update my reading list.

I moved toward my desk and plopped into the creaky, wooden chair. Then, I looked down, thumbing the small, square-cut diamond on my ring finger. Tiny silver sparkles shot out in all directions as the stone glinted under flickering fluorescent lights.

It felt cold.

I felt cold.

Maybe that was partly the chill left over in the office from last night. 'Tween season during November in southwest Florida could flip-flop from frosty at night to fiery during the day and, right now, it seemed downright nippy. Too lazy to turn up the thermostat, I hugged my gray sweater closer around me and flipped open the lid of my high-test, heavy-duty, jumbo java, bought at the island center convenience store.

A blast of earthy dark roast hit me. *Aah.*

Taking a long drink of the steaming liquid, I wondered how it was possible that I, Mallie Monroe, the girl voted "least likely to match two socks" in high school, was ready to actually settle down.

Sure, I'd had a string of temporary jobs before I worked my way south to Mango Bay near the tip of Florida and, while I didn't want to become a nomad again, I also didn't want to morph into some tropical version of a desperate housewife.

I shuddered—not from the cold, this time.

Quickly, I transferred the ring to my right hand, twisted the diamond out of sight and pushed all thoughts of my recent, sudden engagement to Cole Whitney out of my head.

I *really* needed Sandy and her comforting shoulder to lean on—or at least access to one of those self-help websites where she could find an answer to my misguided attempts to understand life. *Damn.* Taking another deep swig of my coffee, I shuffled my Birkenstocks along the floor, slowing spinning my chair in a circle; it creaked and groaned with every rotation.

After a dozen spins, I halted and checked the "Island Time" clock on the wall. Almost ten.

Where the heck was Anita?

Well . . . I guess I really *had* bottomed out; I was now missing my mean-as-a-snake editor who trashed practically every sentence of my stories—even after two years of my working up to the Senior Reporter on our island weekly paper. Actually, I was the *only* reporter working at the *Observer* so, yesterday, I'd secretly given myself the new byline that stated, "Mallie Monroe—Senior Reporter." It had kind of a nice ring to it, especially because Anita didn't know yet. Smiling, I could hardly wait to see what she thought of my byline "promotion" when she saw this week's edition. The *Observer*'s cheapskate owner, Mr. Benton, probably wouldn't mind, so long as the title was in name only. He wasn't known as "Nickel and Dime Benton" for nothing.

But Anita wouldn't like it.

Hey, it was about time I got some kind of recognition for my stint at the *Observer.* After all, I'd lasted more than twenty-four months on the same job.

A milestone.

And the longest period I'd ever stayed with the same employer. Remarkably, I hadn't done anything too run-me-out-of-town dumb. Of course, being involved in four murder investigations and risking my life multiple times might not have been the smartest things, but they'd forced me to display some grit and learn a few tricks of the investigative journalist trade.

Yep, bestowing the title of "Senior Reporter" on myself was more than warranted.

Not that early November on the island would bring more than the usual Fall Fish Toss story or Ladies' Garden Club Gala story. But, hey, you never know. Known mostly as a fishing Mecca, Coral Island stretched north and south, which meant it didn't have that long stretch of powdery white shoreline that kept the tourists coming back year after year. Still, we paralleled the more famous beachy spots when summer had faded, the mid-year vacationers had vamoosed, and the winter snowbirds had yet to migrate to southwest Florida. Season was over.

Too bad that also meant no decent news until the holiday season.

Yawning, I flipped open my cell phone to see if Sandy had texted again.

Nothing from her—but Cole had texted twice with a "thinking about my favorite redhead" post from his photo assignment on a shrimp boat.

I answered with an emoticon, hoping the smiley face would convey what I couldn't express in words.

At least—not yet.

I fingered the ring again.

Would I feel the same way if sexy island cop Nick Billie had given me the ring?

Whoa.

Where did that thought come from?

Instantly, I straightened in my chair, snatched the diamond off my finger, and shoved it into a desk drawer.

I couldn't take this much soul searching before lunchtime; my normal morning decisions included, at best, a debate over ordering a classic or chocolate Krispy Kreme donut on my way to work. That was more than enough.

Just then the front door of the office banged open. I looked up and beheld a middle-aged woman with long strands of overly-bleached blond hair and feathery lines around her tanned face. She wore a long, splashy, tropical-print dress with a seashell necklace and armfuls of bangles. Attractive in an islandly way—except for the wild expression in her eyes. "Someone is trying to kill everything I love," she exclaimed.

I rose to my feet in eager anticipation.

At last—a story!

She made a beeline toward me. "Are you a reporter?"

I held out my hand. "Mallie Monroe—Senior Reporter for the *Observer.*"

Ignoring my hand, she slapped her beringed fingers on my desk. "This is an outrage, and I need the media to get to the bottom of it."

"Of course. Just let me take down your details first," I responded quickly, hunting around for something to write on. All I could find was the crumpled hoagie wrapper—it would have to do. I snatched up a ballpoint pen. "Give me your name, address, and . . . uh, whatever else you know."

She raised a hand to her forehead and gave a little moan.

"Oh, please, take a seat and let me get you a glass of water." I sprinted around my desk, grabbed a plastic chair, and scooted it next to her. She immediately collapsed into the seat, dropping her head into her hands. While the distraught woman continued to moan, I managed to find an unopened water bottle in Sandy's mini-fridge.

"Here you go." I tapped the woman on the shoulder, and she raised her head. "Just try to calm down and compose yourself. We'll take it slowly."

After taking a long swig of water, she closed her eyes for a few moments. The moaning amped down a notch.

Eyelids fluttering open, she took in a deep breath. "I'm Liz Ellis and I live in Paradisio, where I run a small nursery. I've lived there for almost ten years and have never had a single problem—not with my clients and not with my neighbors. For God's sake, I'm a founding member of the Triple P—the Paradisio Planters and Pickers—our organization that supports all of the local island growers." She puffed out her ample chest in pride. "And I donate generously to local charities. Who would want to kill anything or anybody I care about?" She looked up at me with a tortured expression.

"I don't know, Ms. Ellis."

Lips trembling, she sniffed.

Moving back to the chair behind my desk, I retrieved the ballpoint pen and hoagie wrapper. "Now if you could take me through exactly who you think is trying to kill—"

"I'm Liz Ellis. No one hates me." Her voice rose as she thumped the water bottle on my desk top. "No one!"

"Gotcha." I doodled her name on the hoagie wrapper along with the words: *Someone hates her.*

"As for the rest, I'm just not going to stand by and do nothing while I watch the slow march to death around me."

I clicked the pen with an involuntary spasm. "Can't say I blame you, but could we move on to the facts? Are you saying that you witnessed a possible murder?"

She nodded with a quick jerk of her head.

"All right, let's take it from the beginning. Who was killed and when did you see it happen—"

"Not a person, you dimwit—my plants and trees. Someone is deliberately killing all of the organic greenery in my nursery—everything from the bougainvillea bushes to the pygmy palms. They're withering and *dying*—and with them, my business." Her face crumpled into an expression of agony.

Oh.

Herbicide.

"So that's why you're here today? To report a possible plant killer?"

She nodded.

"And no one threatened *you*?"

She shook her head.

I set down the pen and threw the hoagie wrapper in the trash. Then I slipped my business card across the desk. "Here's my card and e-mail address if you need to contact me, but you might want to report this one to the island police. I'm sure Detective Billie will want to do a full investigation—"

"You're just sluffing me off." She shook her finger at me and leaned in until her face was mere inches from mine. *Alcohol breath.* "And you'll be sorry, trust me. I'm Liz Ellis, and I don't like being trifled with—especially when it comes to my nursery."

"Ms. Ellis, I'm not 'sluffing' or 'trifling,' but is it conceivable that your plants are just . . . unhealthy?"

Her mouth dropped open. "Now you're insulting me?"

"No, no. Not at all—"

She spewed an unprintable curse and stomped out of the office, slamming the door behind her.

I blinked, trying to take in what had just happened. The woman was cray-cray.

Fishing the hoagie wrapper out of the trash, I added to my previous doodle: *I hate Liz Ellis.* Then, I tossed it in the can again.

And so much for the big story of the day.

I flipped on my ancient Dell desktop PC (now refurbished) and logged onto the newspaper's system to see if Anita had filed an assignment for me. I scanned my e-mail and found—nothing. I blinked and sat back, shoving my sweater sleeves above my pale, freckled arms (matching my pale, freckled face); then, I checked through the "Trash" section just in case I had mistakenly deleted her message.

Still nothing.

Odd.

I drummed my fingers on the desk and stared at the computer screen, wondering if this editorial evasiveness was some new ploy of Anita's to get me to generate more sensationalized stories.

Could she be that devious?

Is pasta the national dish of Italy?

I clicked on my Inbox again, and saw two new e-mails from local residents who wanted me to cover the closing of a bankrupt septic cleaning company (yuk), and the opening of a new bakery: Sugar and Spice (yum). I responded to the second e-mail and logged the upcoming December date into my online calendar, even though I knew Anita wouldn't be too juiced about it.

She hated heartwarming, community-interest articles—fitting, because she had no heart. Her years as a reporter for the *Detroit Free Press* had apparently eliminated any slight tendency she might've had to connect with another human being on an emotional level. And all those experiences in her youth left me with the middle-aged, nit-picking boss-from-hell: my mentor.

I checked my Inbox again, e-mailed Anita—then waited, and waited, and waited.

A message popped up—from guess who? Liz Ellis.

A plant killer is loose on Coral Island, and you just missed your chance to stop him. Whatever happens is on your head, and I'll make sure you pay. Oh, and by the way, I won't be buying any future advertising with the Observer. *Liz.*

Damn. That last one might hurt. If Mr. Benton got wind of a dissatisfied customer, my new Senior Reporter title could be in jeopardy.

I punched the delete button on her e-mail, making a mental note to ask Sandy to smooth over the troubled waters—and get Liz back in the fold of paying advertisers.

Sipping my coffee once more, I reviewed my options to get cracking on my day's stories. I could call Anita's cell phone, but I was supposed to do that only in an extreme emergency. Imminent death or dismemberment probably qualified—not boredom. I could call her at home, but even after two years on the job I didn't know her home number. As a last resort, I could send her a smoke signal; unfortunately, I didn't have so much as a book of matches, and I'd probably get arrested because we'd had an early season outbreak of brushfires.

I tucked my curls behind my ears, stretched out my jeans-clad legs, and stared down at the nearly empty cup. What else could I do?

Take charge. You're now the Senior Reporter.

I'd ransack Anita's office for any hard-copy assignment sheets she might've left behind yesterday. That way, I could get started before she showed up for work—and distract myself from this mind-numbing *ennui* before I called Liz to follow up on the herbicide.

Rising to my feet, I peered out the front window—just to make certain Anita wasn't making a late appearance in the parking lot. No sign of her recently acquired Buick Century with the crooked bumper (she'd backed into someone months ago and never had it fixed). I was an amateur "car shrink" with, if I say so myself, an uncanny ability to psychoanalyze people according to the type of vehicle they drove. Anita's ramshackle

Buick spoke volumes about her lack of interest in status (and poor depth perception).

Giving the lot one last sweeping glance, I smiled. The coast was clear, so to speak.

I tiptoed into Anita's office, weaving a crooked path around the stacks of ancient *Observer* newspapers, out-of-date phone books (who keeps those in this age of Facebook and Twitter?), and used Official Reporter Notepads. Some of the paper products were so old, the pages had yellowed and curled on the corners. Aside from Anita's other charming qualities, she possessed the "packrat" gene.

When I reached the dented, metal, L-shaped desk, I began to rifle through the heaps of junk on top. Broken stapler. My nail file that had disappeared a month ago. A copy of *Weight Watchers* magazine in which Sandy had pasted her own face on the cover model—one of her sweetly funny weight-loss techniques—except that Anita had drawn a mustache on her. Jeez.

I kept digging, but no assignment sheets turned up.

Baffled, I checked the top drawer and found only two unused jars of bee cream (but that's another story: check out *Killer Kool*), one of which I pocketed as payment for the loss of my nail file. Scanning the bookcase, I turned up a moldy cheese sandwich and crumpled Kleenex.

What a pig sty.

Frustrated and empty-handed, I spied a manila envelope taped to Anita's phone; she'd scrawled my name on it.

Cautiously, I opened it, sliding out a small piece of paper with a handwritten note:

Mallie:

Benton and I decided to elope last night; we're going to honeymoon in Detroit, so he can see the steel mills where I grew up.

How romantic.

I won't be at work all week, so you're in charge while I'm gone.

Don't screw up.

Anita Benton.

My mouth dropped open.

Was it possible? Anita married the middle-aged cheapo owner of the newspaper, the guy who had a pot belly and ear hair and the first dollar he ever earned?

Then, an even more disturbing thought occurred to me: *I'm in charge.*

My legs gave out and I collapsed into Anita's desk chair. One of the wheels promptly fell off, and the chair tilted to one side, causing me to tumble onto the floor—still clutching the letter.

I hit the hard surface with a thud.

After I hyperventilated under Anita's desk for a short while (and scarfed down an unopened Snickers bar that had fallen on the floor), I fantasized madly about packing up my Airstream and teacup poodle and heading to Key West. It was the southernmost point of the U.S., and about as far south as I could go and still remain in the country. Cheeseburger in paradise territory and the last stop on the Mallie Express to Freedom. There was just one problem: I had a life here, including a newly acquired fiancé. Giving myself a quick mental shake, I vowed that I wouldn't run away under any circumstances.

But I needed help—fast.

Stumbling into the main office, I called Cole; he didn't answer. Then, I speed-dialed my great-aunt Lily, the doyenne of Coral Island; my call went straight to voice mail. In desperation, I punched in Sandy's number with a shaky hand.

"Hi, Mallie," she sang out. "You'll never guess where we are right now: a romantic horse-drawn carriage that looks like something out of a fairy tale—"

"Thank goodness you picked up, Sandy," I cut in with a rush of relief. "I'm sorry to call when you're still on your honeymoon, but I came into the office this morning, and no one was here. You know how Anita is always at her desk at the crack of dawn—but not today. I waited and waited, then some woman came in about a plant killer, but she was a nutcase. Anyway, I went into Anita's office and found a note—" I broke off, realizing that the shock had driven my motor mouth into hyperdrive.

"She didn't . . . fire you?" Sandy's tone turned up a notch in seriousness and volume, but I could still hear the steady, reassuring clip-clop of horse hoofs in the background.

"No—worse. She and Benton . . . *eloped,*" I barely managed to eke out the words without getting nauseous.

"What?" Sandy screamed. The horse whinnied.

Wincing, I jerked the phone away from my ear.

"You've got to be kidding me." She lowered her voice a notch. "I mean—they hung out a while back at the Twin Palms, and I'd heard they were spotted at that dumpy restaurant, Le Sink, but . . . married?"

"It's true," I responded, pressing the phone back to the side of my head. "And it gets even more bizarre: She left *me* in charge."

"No way."

"Oh, yeah—way." I echoed her disbelief. "I've got to do interviews and write the stories for this week; then, I'll need to edit copy for the whole paper—and make certain we don't lose any advertisers. Cripes, I'm breaking out in hives just thinking about it." My skin tended to react to everything: the sun, the moon—and especially emotional stress. If not blotchy, red patches, I could feel a hundred new freckles break out across my face, and I already had a humongous amount of them on my forehead, cheeks, and chin.

"Stay calm," Sandy advised, regaining the composure in her voice. "Jimmy, could you please have the driver stop the horse, so I can think?"

"Sure thing, sweetheart." Jimmy's voice answered in the background and, instantly, the sound of the horse hoofs ceased.

A twinge of guilt nagged at me over interrupting the newlyweds, but this was survival. Still clutching the cell phone, I seated myself again at my desk and did a couple of deep breathing techniques and my "muggatoni mantra" that I'd learned in Tae Kwon Do classes. It was my calming chant, my salvation in times of stress, and one of my favorite pastas. It worked—sort of. At least, I didn't feel like I was going to pass out. The sense of imminent doom lingered, though.

"Mallie? Are you with me?" Sandy said.

"Barely." I leaned my head back and closed my eyes briefly.

"That's a start. Okay, here's what you do: check the *Observer*'s archive for last year's editions for this time of year and see what stories you covered. That way, you've got a starting point for this week's articles that cycle every year."

"Great idea," I enthused—then paused, scratching my head. "Why didn't I think of that?"

"You're still in shock over Anita and Benton—it boggles the mind." I could feel her virtual shudder across the miles.

"All right, back to business: review the community calendar and the assignment sheets filed online from last year. After that, you need to get in a temp to help you with the proofs—"

"A copy editor?"

"Get real." She gave a short laugh. "You work for a weekly paper that pays minimum wage—hardly enough for a *photocopy*. But ask around and maybe you'll find someone willing to help out with reading the proofs."

Clicking on the Internet Yellow Pages, I felt a tiny glow of hope stir inside of me. "Which temp service do you use?"

"Service?" Another laugh; this time it sounded more like a chortle. "Start calling anyone who's ever freelanced for us—and beg, beg, beg." The horse whinnied again. Maybe he could write an equine exposé.

I was officially losing it.

"Call Mom," Jimmy urged. "She's a terrific writer."

I almost gagged. Aside from being the island's phony freelance psychic, Madame Geri wrote our monthly Astrology Now! column—but that hardly qualified her as a journalist. "I can't call her—she's trouble with a capital *T.* After all the tight spots and near disasters she's got me involved in *outside* of work, God knows what would happen if she were actually working in the office." Actually, "tight spots" was an understatement; Madame Geri almost caused my death several times with her pushing me to act on her half-baked predictions. "Give me some other names of possible temps."

"Easier said than done." Sandy paused. "When you're asking for the ability to write a complete sentence, it kinda thins the pool."

"Think!"

"Madame Geri is your only choice, unless . . ." She paused again, this time longer. "I've got a brilliant idea, but you probably won't like it."

"I'm hanging by a thread here—"

"How 'bout Anita's sister, Bernice?"

I grimaced.

"Before you say anything, remember she ran the *Observer* when Anita took off on vacation—"

"Poorly," I said, gritting my teeth as the memories of Bernice's short tenure as editor came back to me.

"Come on. She managed the paper for a week, and it didn't fold. Aside from her obsession with selling advertising, she wasn't half bad doing Anita's job."

"Are you kidding? She used to call me 'Miss Priss' when I wouldn't wear tacky t-shirts with our advertisers' names on them. Give me a break. I'm a journalist and shouldn't have had to wear an 'Eat Me at The Frozen Flamingo' t-shirt."

"Think of her as . . . 'eccentric'." Sandy added something under her breath to Jimmy that I couldn't make out.

"Hah." The only good thing I could say about Bernice was, unlike my skinny, leathery boss, she'd never smoked. That's something, I guess.

"Come on, give her a try," Sandy urged.

We continued to argue as I lifted my gaze to the ceiling in futile hope for divine intervention.

As if on cue, Madame Geri strolled through the door with her turquoise parrot, Marley, on her shoulder. My eyes widened as I took in her houndstooth, retro, fitted jacket and skirt, complemented by her grayish dreadlocks tucked into a fifties'-style fedora. She looked like a combo of Rosalind Russell and Madonna—a new age "Girl Friday" who was Desperately Seeking Sanity.

"I'm here to help," she pronounced.

"You called her," I hissed in the cell phone at Sandy and Jimmy. *That's* what Sandy had been murmuring to Jimmy. "Traitors!"

"Au contraire." Madame Geri tipped her brim. "The spirit world contacted me to let me know you were all alone in the office, panicked—with death and disaster on the way."

I raised my brows in disbelief on both counts.

A flattering comparison, indeed.

"It doesn't matter why I came here. The important thing is I'm ready to take on my first big story." She produced a mini-laptop and dog-eared book from her black, faux-alligator bag: *The Dummy's Guide to Journalism.* "And, by the by, the spirit world never makes a mistake: you can be sure that a death is imminent, and *I'm* going to write about it."

Journalism 101 just hit the skids.

Chapter Two

"Okay, let me explain," I began, working hard to maintain my patience after Sandy and Jimmy's betrayal. "Journalists write stories on events that have actually *happened*—with verifiable sources. And the 'spirit world' doesn't qualify as a 'source'."

"Oh, it's going to happen all right, whether you believe it or not," she responded matter-of-factly, flipping through her *Dummy's Guide.*

"The answer is—*no.*" Easing back in my chair with a careful balancing over the wheels, I folded my hands in a pyramid shape over my lap. "Do you have anything *concrete* for me?"

"Oh, yeah. I've got a great lead on a front-page item that will do nicely until the real action starts with the murder."

"Look, I've already heard about herbicide this morning, so I guess your story can't be any worse . . . until the upcoming *homicide* occurs, of course—pardon my sarcasm."

"Three cheers for Madame Geri, who's going to save the *Observer.*" Sandy's shout erupted from my cell phone. I'd forgotten that it was open and, instantly, snapped the device shut.

"What's the 'scoop'?" I asked, bracing myself.

She slipped a four-by-six color photo out of the *Guide* and held it in front of my face.

I studied the image of a tattooed, spiky-haired young guy holding up what appeared to be some kind of dilapidated . . . violin with a faded finish and missing strings.

"So?"

"Can't you see it?" She pointed at the musical instrument in the picture. "The image of Abraham Lincoln is imprinted on the violin—right above the chin rest," she explained, her index finger tracing what appeared to be a series of circular scratches on the old wood. "You can clearly make out Abe's gaunt cheeks, the beard, and the sad expression. It's a historical miracle!"

I squinted. "Just don't see it."

"Not even the famous stovepipe hat?" She rapped the picture repeatedly. "You can't tell me *that* isn't clear—"

"As mud," I quipped, still trying to detect the Great Emancipator's features. All I could make out was a bunch of squiggly scratches. "Maybe I need glasses, but a violin with some funny marks on it isn't exactly front-page headline material."

"Maybe you should go right to bifocals." Madame Geri lowered the picture with a shake of her head.

"Just because I can't see an imaginary outline of Abe Lincoln on a beat-up violin?"

"Bite your tongue about the sixteenth president of the United States," she warned, her tone upping a notch in volume, which caused Marley to flutter his wings. I kept a wary eye on that bird; he didn't like me, and I didn't like him. Mutual disdain. "Joe Earl Chapman bought the violin off eBay—it was listed as an 'artifact' by a certified music historian in Boston."

"More like certifiable," I muttered under my breath as I kept my distance from Marley's long talons. "Unless I heard Abe Lincoln himself say it was his picture, I wouldn't believe it."

"Okay, I'll verify it," she said, her mouth curving into a smug smile as she stroked the parrot. I swear he purred.

"*Please* don't tell me that you're in actual communication with Old Abe?"

"None other—and he's a great man, even in death." She closed her eyes and began humming.

"Stop!" I jerked forward in my chair and held up my hands in defeat. "Do the story on the violin, but I don't want to hear any more talk about communing with Lincoln right here in the *Observer* office; it's creeping me out."

Her eyes flew open and the humming ceased. "*No problema.* I'll get started on the interview with Joe Earl right away." She seated herself at Sandy's desk and transferred Marley to a temporary perch on the stack of bridal magazines that Sandy had left in the office. As soon as the beady-eyed bird was settled with a last tender pat, Madame Geri cracked open the *Dummy's Guide* again. "First, I'll read up on 'The Ten Tips to a Front-page Feature,' and, then, I'll call Joe Earl."

I opened my mouth to remind her to take interview notes, but my cell phone rang, and I turned my attention to the number: Sandy the Traitor. I let the call go to voice mail.

"I like Tip Number One." Madame Geri rubbed her chin meditatively. "It suggests citing a classic quote in the article's first paragraph . . . I think I'll use the Emancipation Proclamation. That's a winner."

"Sounds good." What was the point in giving my new "reporter" any advice? She'd do what she wanted no matter what I said. I'd let her write the story, and then I'd edit the hell (and craziness) out of it.

Yikes. I was starting to sound like . . . Anita.

Quickly, I turned back to my computer and scanned through the *Observer* articles from last November. Something else *had* to turn up—I couldn't rely on a bogus Lincoln violin for newspaper copy.

After an hour of wading through the mush of last year's autumn-themed stories, I found nothing more exciting than a "Growing Greens" gardening workshop led by a woman who harvested herbs out of carved pumpkins. I didn't even remember writing it.

Resting my chin on my hand, I fixated on the computer screen with a sinking feeling that the certified Old Abe violin might really end up being front-page material this week. *Unbelievable.* Needless to say, Anita would have my hide when she returned, if that's all I'd managed to eke out for a headline. Not only would I have to wave bye-bye to my new title of Senior Reporter, I wouldn't have a chance in hell of ever being in charge of more than the office deli order in the future.

I opened my desk drawer and checked on the engagement ring, which still rested quietly amid the paperclips and Post-Its. A good thing, too, because I might end up as a stay-at-home bride if I couldn't get out a good edition of the *Observer* this week.

"Anita won't fire you," Madame Geri commented as she clicked the keys on her laptop, nestled her cell phone between her right ear and shoulder, and kept the *Dummy's Guide* propped open with the elbow.

Who knew she could multi-task like the Wizard of Oz? Even more importantly, how could she read my thoughts like that?

Then again, it might have something to do with my doodling pictures of myself with a hangman's noose around my neck, along with the caption "Please don't let Anita fire me."

"Hang tough, Mallie."

"Sure." I began scrolling through last year's *Observer*'s stories one more time.

She hitched the cell phone closer to her mouth. "Hi, Joe Earl. This is Madame Geri, and I need your help. I'm filling in as a temporary reporter at the *Observer* and wanted to write a story about your famous violin. I know you're probably slammed with your online business, but could you spare some time for an interview—"

"Eureka!" I exclaimed.

Madame Geri lowered the phone. "Pipe down, *please.*"

"I can't believe that I overlooked something right in front of my face. It must be the trauma of being left in charge." I raised my hands, palms up, in triumph. "It's town-council election year. That's our front-page news!"

She covered the bottom of her cell phone with her fingers. "A small-time island election is hardly in the same category as the Abe Lincoln Violin. Get your priorities straight, Mallie." She emphasized each of the last three words with disdain. "Joe Earl's story might even go national if we do it right."

"Guess so, if it's picked up by the kind of rag that publishes stories about people being abducted by six-toed aliens." I waved my hand in a gesture of dismissal. "The town-council election is our headline."

"Local yokel election? What a bore." Bernice Sanders stood at the door.

Uh-oh.

My caution turned to disbelief as I took in her "new look." Bernice had traded her tacky nautical garb for a shoulder-length blond wig, white, leather mini-dress, and platform shoes—topped off by twin silver snake bracelets that wrapped around each forearm. "How do you like my outfit? It's my new Lady Gaga get-up."

"Stunning," Madame Geri enthused.

"Uh . . . I'm speechless." I had to give her kudos for donning skintight leather when she was on the down side of sixty.

"Too cute, huh?" Bernice twirled around to give us a view from all angles. "Now that Anita married that moron, Benton, I realized she'd be flaunting the old coot in my face till I was hooked up with a guy, too. So I updated my look and got on a 'Singles over Sixty' online dating group. So far, I've had ten hits." She grinned. "Can you believe that *I'm* not married when my butt-ugly twin is enjoying wedded bliss?"

"Go figure," I agreed, still mesmerized by the vision of her slightly plump body and saggy knees emphasized by the short hemline.

"I stopped by 'cause Sandy just called me and said you needed an extra hand while Anita's gone."

Double traitor.

Madame Geri nodded and motioned her over to our desks. Then, she raised the phone to her ear and finally resumed her conversation with Joe Earl.

After leveling a glare at Madame Pseudo-Psychic, I turned back to Bernice. "It's fine, really. We have it under control."

"Don't be a dork, Miss Priss. There's nothing wrong with admitting you're in over your head," Bernice said as she strolled in our direction. "And let's not forget that I edited this sorry excuse for a newspaper for over a week—"

"Your biggest executive decision was to put a tree stump in the middle of the office to get the owner to buy advertising," I reminded her, seething at the all-too-familiar "Miss Priss" misnomer.

"It worked, didn't it?" She placed one hand on her hip and assumed the "teacup" Hollywood posture. "The client bought half-page ads—with color, no less. That dope sister of mine has never understood that money drives the media, just like everything else in this world."

I hated to admit it, but she had a point. Her marketing tactics *had* attracted bucks like termites to wood (literally, in the case of the stump) and the *Observer* couldn't survive without the advertising dollars.

"Sis might have Benton bankrolling her, but every gravy train derails at some point," she continued with a sage nod, adjusting her bracelets. "When the honeymoon glow wears off and her new hubby reverts to *el cheapo bosso* again, she might find herself struggling to keep this dumpy newspaper afloat."

I wasn't sure if I was more alarmed at the thought of the

newspaper being in financial distress or Anita enjoying any type of "glow" with Mr. Benton.

"My sister's lack of vision aside," Bernice said. "I was a good manager/editor then, and I'll be an even better reporter now."

Chewing my lower lip with uncertainty, I eyed Madame Geri's face, kindled with animation as she questioned Joe Earl. "Do you think there might be an Abe thumbprint on the frets?"

I heard a mumbled answer emit from her phone.

Was that going to be my headline after all?

Bernice followed my glance, and a self-satisfied expression appeared on her face. "You know I'm your best shot right now."

Still, I hesitated. Could anyone have predicted that the office staff would decline so quickly into this motley duo?

"All right," I said, finally giving in.

"Smokin'!" She rubbed her hands together and smacked her lips as she headed toward the back of the office. "First thing, we need some heat in here—it's freezing."

Marley squawked, and they eyed each other as if weighing an opponent for potential combat. Glances locked, Bernice edged around him on her way to the thermostat, never turning her back to him. Eventually, *she* was the one to break off the stare-fest. I swear that damned parrot puffed out his chest and preened in smug delight.

"Icksnay, ArleyMay," she quipped in her best Pig Latin after cranking up the furnace. "What's that collar around his neck?"

Madame Geri mouthed "pet pager" silently.

"She likes to keep tabs on him, even though he rarely leaves her side," I said, tossing an Official Reporter's Notepad in my hobo bag; it disappeared in the jumble of gum, pens, and cherry Chap Stick. I liked to travel heavy. "By the way, Anita doesn't like the temperature above sixty-five degrees. It costs too much, and Mr. Benton reviews the electric bill personally every month."

"I'm not working in an igloo when I've got a big story to write." Bernice flipped the long strands of her wig and turned back towards me. "So, do you want to hear my blockbuster news story or what?"

I opened my mouth to answer, but Bernice kept going. " 'Bicycle Bandit Strikes Again.' Here's what happened: two Schwinn bikes were lifted right off my neighbors' lanai over the weekend—in broad daylight. Then, this morning a kid's training wheels went missing. So, I'm calling him the 'bicycle bandit.' Home run of a headline, huh?"

Oh, yeah. Pulitzer Prize all the way.

Madame Geri finally hung up on the Joe Earl conversation. "More like a foul ball compared to my story. Take a look at this." She thrust the photo of Joe Earl and his tattered violin in Bernice's face.

"Well, I'll be damned." Her heavily made-up eyes widened. "As I live and breathe. Abe Lincoln."

"Not you, too?" Shaking my head, I sprinted for the door before I could hear another word of nuttiness.

"You know, I've got a shriveled-up mango in my fridge that's the spittin' image of George Washington," Bernice said.

Too late.

While driving to the town-hall meeting at the north end of Coral Island, I took the opportunity to clear my mind of everything I had just heard over the last thirty minutes. Then I repeated my "muggatoni mantra" again for good measure in case I had a flashback. Unfortunately, chanting about pasta only made me hungry, so I had to hit the island Dairy Queen drive-thru for a burger—with fries.

Luckily, I was one of those skinny-minnie body types that rarely gained weight. Unfortunately, I also had the flat chest to go with it. *Metabolism karma.*

Once I'd downed the mouth-watering fast food, I resumed my calming mantra on a full stomach and headed north on Cypress Drive—the island's main drag—hoping against hope that this election story would be exciting enough for a headline.

My ancient Ford truck, affectionately named Rusty (for obvious reasons), chugged along as I kept reminding myself that I'd learned a lot from Anita over the last two years, and I could turn a tree planting into front-page material. And there was always the Abe Lincoln feature or the bicycle-bandit headline to fill in the gap if I bottomed out.

I promptly rammed down the gas pedal and hit Rusty's maximum speed of fifty-five mph.

My cell phone rang, and I checked the number: Sandy the Traitor.

I flipped it open. "How could you do this to me? You and Jimmy called the last two people I'd ever want working at the *Observer:* Madame Geri and Bernice. They barged into the office like they owned it. Even worse, they came up with some half-baked stories on a bicycle bandit and a haunted violin—"

"You mean Joe Earl's Abe Lincoln fiddle?"

I could hear the awe in her voice and rolled my eyes.

"Mallie, that will make a great headline. I've seen it, and Abe's face is all over that violin. It's eerie."

Groaning, I hung up on her for the second time that day. My fingers clenched on the steering wheel. As Senior Reporter, I knew I could find a lead on something better than what those two had in mind.

The bankrupt septic-cleaning company was looking better and better as a possible lead story.

Almost at the point where Cypress Drive dead-ended on Coral Island Sound, I spied the familiar town-hall building where I'd attended numerous council meetings: a raised, wooden structure, with lattice work covering the lower part and an exterior painted sea-foam green. Tall royal palm trees fanned both sides of the front stairs in an arching embrace, sweeping fronds just barely touching the roof. The whole ambience breathed a laid-back tropical feel, but the real truth was the actual council gatherings generally consisted of endless discussions on bike-path repairs, zoning ordinances, and road maintenance. Major tedium—but the bread and butter of every small-town reporter's stories.

I couldn't zone out completely during the meetings, but I did spend a lot of my time daydreaming about cracking a hard-hitting story that had some teeth to it.

Pulling into the parking lot, Jimmy Buffet's song "A Pirate Looks at Forty" wafted out, and I couldn't resist a grin. Everyone in the town hall had passed the midlife milestone long ago—with nary a pirate in sight. I clicked off the engine and Rusty responded with a backfire of smoke accompanied by a wicked rattle before going silent.

My truck had seen that age, too.

Jogging up the steps, I dropped the truck keys in my bag and pulled out my notepad.

"Hey, Mallie. You're a dollar short and day late—typical." Everett Jacobs, the island's resident curmudgeon, limped past me on his cane. Quickly, I swerved to the side since he was known to smash a toe or two with the rubber tip. He sported his usual outfit of plaid, knee-length shorts, sports shirt, socks, and black wing tips. I'd known him from my early days on the island when I'd been the target of his surly quips, and he hadn't changed much, except he'd become a little more bent since having knee replacement.

"Don't tell me the meeting is over already?" I asked, my heart sinking.

"It is for me," he tossed off, hobbling along. "I couldn't listen to one more word of Travis Harper's and Bucky McGuire's boring garbage talk about 'marketing the island,' or some such nonsense. Those two councilmen wannabees are just plain stupid. The last thing we need are more tourists. I hate 'em."

Relieved I hadn't missed my story chance, I commented, "They do bring money to the island."

"If people lived more frugally, they wouldn't need extra cash." He headed toward his ancient Chevy sedan, parked sideways so he took up two spaces. *Typical.* "I still have my black and white TV, and haven't thrown away a single sandwich baggie in ten years. There's nothing wrong with recycling your own plastic and foil; that stuff is good for years."

Ugh. "Catch you later." Waving him off, I entered the building. The first thing I noticed was the audience section contained the usual twenty people, most of whom were well over seventy, with a Bud Light in hand. Then, I realized they were all riveted on the spectacle before them on the podium: two men and two women sat behind the table, and my great-aunt Lily was positioned in the center, banging a gavel as she shouted, "Order. I will have order." Her comments seemed to be directed at the two men on her left, who were shouting at each other, their faces mere inches apart.

I blinked in amazement. Everett thought *this* scene was boring?

Eagerly I sprinted forward, pen in hand.

I didn't know either of the men, but presumed they were Bucky and Travis: one guy middle-aged, short, with a receding hairline; the other one pushing seventy, tall, with a monk's pate bald spot (at least, they had something in common). The younger one had plastered a couple of hair strands on top of his head in the dreaded comb-over, which looked like limp seaweed glued to his scalp.

"You're full of it, Travis!" Mr. Comb-over spat out in a gravelly voice as he stood up.

"Bucky, I refuse to respond to that type of insulting, unpleasant discourse," the old guy drawled in a southern accent as he rose to his feet, drawing himself to his full height with an indignant tug of his navy sports jacket. "My position on the issue of the island recreational center passes remains unchanged: only residents who live on the island can get permits to use the swimming pool; otherwise, we'll be attracting riffraff from town who want to use our facilities. It just makes plain, good, old-fashioned common sense."

"Crapola!"

Travis's face flushed, but he kept his features composed. "The response of a *small* man."

Bucky thrust out his barrel chest and stomped his high-heeled cowboy boots. "Are you calling me short?"

"If the shoe lift fits . . ." Travis glanced down his patrician nose as if beholding some type of insect.

"All right, that's it." Bucky held up his arms and curled his hands into fists. "We're going outside to settle this, man to man."

A few spectators urged them on by raising their Buds and murmuring a chorus of "Do it!"

"Fine." Travis began to shrug out of his well-fitted, navy jacket. "I'm warning you that I was a Golden Gloves boxer in college."

"Big deal." Bucky sneered.

Aunt Lily finally rose to her feet, gavel still in hand. "No one is going anywhere. This is an election, not a prize fight. And you two should be ashamed of this display. There are children in the audience, for goodness sake." She pointed the mallet at a young girl with braided hair and sweet, delicate features drawn tight with fear. "What's the matter with the two of you?"

The crowd murmured in abashed agreement.

"*He* started it," Bucky said.

"I did not," Travis replied.

"It doesn't matter." Aunt Lily leveled her doyenne-of-the-island stern glance at both of them. "Just sit down and stick to the election issues, or I'll have Sam deal with you." She nodded in the direction of the island's Zen handyman who worked for her and looked like Gandhi on steroids: shaved head, pierced ear, and rope-like muscles on his forearms. He also had a black belt in Tae Kwon Do.

Sam had taught me how to do a roundhouse kick, how to punch through plywood, and how to use my mantra in times of stress. *My sensei.*

He stood up; he didn't need to do more.

Bucky and Travis immediately sat down.

I tried not to react, but my lips curved upwards almost of their own volition.

My great-aunt was formidable—in a genteel sort of way—but, with Sam at her side, she could take over a small nation. Petite and still slim in her "golden years" (no age, please), she possessed the same red hair that had been passed on to me, except hers had dimmed from the color of a fire engine to a faded hydrant. But her freckles still stood out vividly against her porcelain complexion, and her eyes shone as brightly blue. I adored her.

"I'm the chair of this town council, and I intend to get this meeting back on track!" She shook a finger at Travis and Bucky, but then flashed a little wink in my direction. "If you two can't behave like adults, I'll have you thrown out of here and your candidacy declared null and void."

They both hung their heads in wordless submission. Sam eased back down and quiet descended on the room.

"Now, let's resume our debate—with no more temper tantrums, please." Aunt Lily slid into her chair once more with a graceful glide and rapped the gavel on the wooden block. "As

"There's nothing wrong with these fish. They've been in my truck only a few hours."

"In a cooler?" Wanda Sue pressed as she picked up a fish and sniffed it.

"Nah." Bucky waved his hand in dissent. "Just wrapped 'em in the *Observer,* but it was some kind of outdoorsy story, so it's okay."

That would be my "Edible Seed" article from last week.

Wanda Sue shook her head and tossed the fish on the table. "I'll pass."

Destiny nudged the fish with her index finger and wrinkled her nose. "I'll pass, too."

Aunt Lily banged her gavel again, while Travis kept spewing insults at Bucky, and Bucky kept handing out tilapia. None of the spectators paid attention to Travis's protestations because they were too occupied in helping themselves to the free fish.

I snapped a picture with my cell phone for my article, filled with reluctant admiration over Bucky's gimmick; he'd found an election loophole that seemed totally inappropriate, but somehow irresistible. I eyed the fish myself; they didn't look half bad for a fry-up.

"All right. I've had enough of this travesty!" Travis grabbed the gavel out of Aunt Lily's hand and began to pound on the fish, causing soggy pieces to fly in all directions.

People ducked and grabbed for their fish.

"Stop it!" Bucky shouted as he seized Travis's arm. "You're smashing 'em to bits."

Travis grinned maniacally and hammered the tilapia even harder. Roaring an expletive and rearing back his arm, Bucky aimed a punch at his opponent's chin. He missed and tipped forward with the force of his intended blow. As he struggled to regain his balance, he rammed an elbow into Travis's stomach, which caused the older man to double over and yelp.

Miraculously, Travis didn't drop the gavel.

I watched in helpless fascination with my fellow islanders (who were now transfixed with the drama) as Travis, from his hunched-over position, swung the gavel against Bucky's legs, rapping him hard on the knees a couple of times. Bucky winced with each blow.

"Call the police," I finally called out to no one in particular as I flipped open my cell phone again. Unfortunately, the battery was now dead.

Uh-oh.

Somebody was going to get hurt.

A few other people pulled out their cell phones again but, instead of punching in 9-1-1, they started video recording the fight and taking selfies with the podium behind them.

I dashed toward the podium, but Sam was already en route ahead of me.

Travis had straightened and was thumping Bucky on the chest with the gavel. Countering with his own attack, Bucky kicked Travis in the shins, causing him to hop from foot to foot, as he tried to evade Bucky's cowboy boot toe pokes. Travis finally dropped the gavel. Instantly, Bucky reached down to retrieve it, but Travis kicked the gavel across the podium out of reach. Snarling, they cuffed, smacked, and pummeled each other with open fists, not doing much damage but managing to knock over the table and scatter the fish all over the floor.

"I'll kill you!" Bucky yelled out.

"I'll kill you first!" Travis retorted.

They wrestled each other to the floor and rolled around, coating each other's clothes in fish guts.

Ick.

"Break it up!" Sam ordered, his shoes slipping on the slimy residue.

"This is just insane." Destiny rose to her feet, holding up her iPhone. "I swear that I'll call the police if you two don't stop the craziness right now! Do you hear me? Bucky? Bucky?" Her voice rose to almost a high-pitched scream as she said his name.

She might as well have been whistling "Dixie" for all the attention they paid to her threat.

Bucky grasped a tilapia carcass and whacked Travis with the tail.

"Help!" I cried out.

Amid the chaos, a flare gun went off and everyone froze.

Chapter Three

"We've got a shooter!" someone yelled out.

I hit the deck, folding my arms around my head in a protective huddle, the hard, cool tile pressing against my face. Everyone else did the same, and the room turned deadly silent as we all waited to see if there would be a second flare.

Arms and legs quivering, I stayed down and held my breath, but no more firings echoed through the room.

Who had done it?

Travis or Bucky?

My heart pounded a terrified staccato in my chest at the thought of either one of those crazy men possessing any type of firearm.

Please don't let them maim or injure me. I'm a bride-to-be!

As my checkered life passed before my eyes (I really needed to deal with this whole "marriage" thing and decide once and for all whether to get a trousseau or new beau), I strained my ears, but didn't hear another shot. Slowly, I tilted my head to the side and peeped one eye open.

Everett lay on his back, clutching his cane to his chest and mumbling curses.

Motioning for him to stay down, I turned my face to the other side and saw Bucky and Travis on the floor of the podium, heads tucked down. Sam had thrown himself over Aunt Lily and held her in a protective embrace. I couldn't help the ghost of a smile; he was always her protector, no matter what.

Then I scanned the rest of the podium and found only one person standing: Wanda Sue, holding a black-handled gun over her head, with the barrel pointed upwards.

A wave of anger surged through me, replacing the fear.

Leaping to my feet, I moved forward and shouted, "What the hell are you doing? You could've hurt someone."

"Whadaya mean?" Wanda Sue looked at the weapon, holding it out with a sheepish grin. "This little ole thing couldn't harm a flea; it's a flare gun."

"It could've still caused a burn wound on someone if you'd missed your mark." I pointed at the ceiling where she had fired the gun. A black, smoky stain had appeared where the flare had drilled into the stuccoed ceiling. "These things can be lethal."

Most of the audience members had risen to their feet and were videotaping the ceiling damage.

"Hey, I was just trying to stop those two numskulls from smashing up things worse; they're plum loco." Wanda Sue stared at the charcoal-colored mark, then shrugged and jammed the weapon back in her large, leather purse. "Okay, so maybe firing a flare gun in the middle of a town-council meeting wasn't the best thing to do, but I couldn't think of any other way to get them to stop beating on each other."

"The bigger question is, what are you doing carrying around a flare gun in your purse?"

"Oh, honey, self-protection." She waved off the question as if I'd asked why she carried lipstick in her bag. "You can't be too careful, even on Coral Island—especially with that bicycle bandit on the loose."

Oh, yeah, a flare gun's going to help.

"Please don't tell Nick Billie. He'll have my hide, for sure."

"He'll probably find out." Sarcasm edged out my anger as I swept my hand across the roomful of amateur videographers.

"Wanda Sue, I intend to take immediate legal action against

you." Travis rose with an ashy-colored face and fish-spattered suit. "For attempted murder." He began to brush off slimy fish scales with an indignant toss of his head.

"Me, too." Bucky had managed to make it to his feet, sweat pouring off his face. "You were aiming for me, you crazy woman!"

"Pffffft." Wanda Sue rolled her eyes. "It was only a warning shot, and I aimed upwards. If I'd wanted to hit you, I would have, trust me."

"That's a confession!" Bucky shouted. "Wanda Sue tried to attack me!"

"Attack?" she scoffed. "That's big talk coming from you after everyone saw you slapping Travis silly with fish guts."

Who could argue with that?

"Witness!" an elderly woman from the audience yelled out. "I caught it all on my cell phone."

Wanda Sue tossed the woman a smile.

Bucky muttered something under his breath as he moved over to where Destiny still sat on the floor.

"I'm calling my lawyer, too," Destiny finally piped up, brushing her hair back from her face with a trembling hand as Bucky helped her stand. "You can't just go around popping off a flare gun. It's against the law."

"Maybe, and maybe not." Wanda Sue dug around in her purse and whipped out a piece of paper. "See this? I've got a permit to carry a concealed weapon. And if I feel threatened, I've got the right to defend myself."

"At a fish fight?" Destiny grabbed her files and clutched them to her chest. "I'm outta here."

"I'm with you," Bucky agreed, then turned to the audience, most of whom were packing up to go. "Let's not all leave on a sour note. I've got more free tilapia in my truck."

Everyone clapped.

"More bribes," Travis said through gritted teeth as he shook the last tilapia bits off his suit sleeves. "I won't have it, I'll tell you."

Aunt Lily snatched up the gavel and banged it on the table once. "This meeting is over!" She sagged against Sam's chest and whispered something for his ears alone. But I could sort of guess at the gist of her words.

"You are *not* giving out any more fish," Travis said.

"Try and stop me," Bucky retorted.

Travis's eyebrows drew together in a thunderous line. "Oh, I will. Make no mistake about that."

Shrugging, Bucky strode to the exit, dogged the whole way by Travis, who kept posing arguments about the illegality of handing out free fish. Several aging islanders trooped out after them, grinning and clutching their cell phones, obviously ready for another photo op. Destiny exited through a side door.

Everett tapped me on the shin with his cane. "I guess the second act starts in the parking lot."

"I'll pass—sounds like it'll be a repeat of act one." Tossing my notepad and pen in my hobo bag, I then heaved it over my shoulder. "In fact, the whole town-council meeting isn't much of a story, but at least Wanda Sue's flare gun spiced it up a bit, even though I almost broke my elbow as I dove for the floor." I rubbed my right arm and winced when I hit the sore spot.

"That's why they say local politics are a battlefield," Everett said as he limped past me, brushing a lone tilapia out of his way with a flick of the cane. "Call me a sentimental fool, but I'm casting one of my votes for Wanda Sue. A woman who carries a flare gun won't take guff from anyone once she's in office. My kind of person. In fact, I might invite her over for a date and fish cook-up."

I guess it was true that politics did, indeed, make strange bedfellows.

★ ★ ★ ★ ★

Half an hour later, I pulled into my beachfront luxury abode at the Twin Palms RV resort. Actually, the "beach" was only a small strip of sand on Coral Island Sound, just about wide enough for a handful of picnic tables, a volleyball net, and an illegal fire pit, all of which had been placed near the surf. And the "luxury" part wasn't exactly true, either. I lived in a refurbished, 4,220-pound, silver Airstream, but it seemed spacious enough for my teacup poodle, Kong, and me. And its massive, submarine-type hull would survive a flood, hurricane, or hailstorm—whichever came first.

As I parked Rusty under my blue and white awning, I took a quick glance at the camping van next door. Cole had parked it there six months ago, proceeded to make a life for himself on Coral Island—and woo me back.

Successfully, I suppose, since now we were engaged.

I swallowed hard and flexed my fingers on the steering wheel.

Oh, no.

My hands were bare.

Panic surged inside of me as I realized that I'd left the diamond ring in my desk drawer at the *Observer* office. *Stupid. Stupid. Stupid.* How could I have left something as valuable as a diamond ring in an unlocked desk? The office woes must've shaken me up more than I thought.

Quickly, I started to shift my truck into reverse, when it occurred to me that it had been almost six hours since Kong had a walk. In all fairness to my pooch, I couldn't drive back to the *Observer* until I had given his tiny bladder a break. After Kong did his thing, I could hotfoot it back to the *Observer,* retrieve my ring, and race back here, without Cole ever knowing the truth about my irresponsible behavior.

There was no sign of life at his campsite, so I figured he was still at his photo shoot for our seasonal mid-island produce stand, Casa de Veggie.

With any luck, my retrieval plan just might work.

Jogging toward my Airstream, I jerked open the trailer's door, and my gray, curly-headed poodle torpedoed into my arms, barking and licking my face as if he hadn't seen me in a year.

Doggie devotion at its best.

"I missed you, too, but I'm in a major rush, Kong." Giving him a quick hug, I plugged in my cell phone to recharge it, then grabbed his leash and fastened it onto his collar. As we headed for the shore, I kept glancing back at Cole's van. Then I noticed a fifth-wheel travel RV had been positioned on the other side of my Airstream: spanking new, with multiple slide-outs and a Toyota Tundra parked in front. I stood there for a few moments, admiring the shiny black RV, with a tropical mural of the Everglades painted on the back, and wondering as to the identity of my new neighbor.

A big-bucks snowbird?

Then I spotted the Dade County Miami license plate and "music freak" decals.

An in-state singer glitterati?

Before I could come up with possible owners for the luxury recreational vehicle, Kong barked in protest and pulled me in the opposite direction from the beach. I uttered a threat and tugged on his leash. After almost two years, he still didn't like the water; but, that's where the sea oats were located—and one of our main options for Kong to find a private spot. Once I reached the sand, I kicked off my Birkenstocks.

"Come on, Kong." Fortunately, his diminutive size made it easy for me to yank him along. As he occupied himself with finding just the right location, I tapped my toes in the sand, feeling the gritty particles against my skin. *Please let Cole's photo perfectionism keep him away a little longer.*

Taking in a few calming breaths and muttering a "muggatoni

mantra" for good measure, I tried to focus on the cool breeze against my face as I gazed out over the Gulf of Mexico. Light, choppy waves were rolling in with the surf. It would probably be high tide tonight as the harvest moon rose and the temperature dropped—a weather roller coaster.

Just like life.

I blinked at the depth of my own self-reflection for the second time in one day.

"Hey, Mallie!" a familiar geriatric voice wafted across the hilly sand dunes between the RV park and the shoreline.

I turned. Pop Pop Welch, the RV park's septuagenarian handyman, hobbled over on his spindly legs and waved something in one hand while wheeling his portable oxygen tank in the other. "I've got your mail. Looks like you got another comic book."

"It's a graphic novel," I exclaimed. Okay, so much for newfound depth. "Hey, a girl on the brink of matrimony needs some light distraction like 'Batgirl: Kicking Assassins'."

Pop Pop grinned, revealing a ghastly set of yellowed dentures, but at least he had them back in place again after losing them in the maintenance shed last week. I won't tell who found them.

"Thanks. Just set the mail on my Airstream steps, please," I said in a loud voice. "Kong is taking his good time to finish his business." Mostly, I didn't want to get into a conversation with him about Cole. A few months ago, I'd taken Pop Pop with me to a couple of restaurants when I was reviewing them as the temporary *Observer* Food Critic. Unfortunately a murder took place at one of the eateries (yet another story) and, even more unfortunately, he still saw himself as my fallback boyfriend. So I tried never to give him the slightest reason to think Cole was anything but a perfect fiancé, but Pop Pop kept trying.

I had to give him points for persistence, but . . . seriously, *dude*.

"Don't forget, I still have discount coupons for our hoagie date at the Circle-K if he leaves you at the altar!" Pop Pop took a whiff of oxygen.

"Will do." I gave him a thumbs-up.

He wheezed a few times and tottered off.

After Kong finally did his thing, I refilled his food and water dishes and zipped back to the *Observer* office, hoping against hope that Bernice was out covering the nefarious bicycle bandit, and that Madame Geri was interviewing Joe Earl about his eerie violin.

I didn't feel like dealing with either of them right now after the uproar at the town hall flare-gun incident and my nail-biting nervousness over the forgotten diamond.

As I pulled into the parking lot, I noticed neither Bernice's nor Madame Geri's vehicle in sight. *Yippee.* I could retrieve my ring with neither of them being the wiser, and I'd even have time to sketch out a short piece on the election antics. It wasn't headline material, but would work nicely as a second-page story.

I let myself into the office and raced right over to my desk.

Yanking open the drawer, I looked down and found—nothing.

The ring was gone.

Shoving back my curls, I frantically sifted through the junk of office supplies in the drawer, pulling out each item one by one and shaking out the stapler box, Scotch tape dispenser, and scissors, hoping that the ring might have miraculously attached itself to one of them and would drop out.

But I came up empty.

Ramming the drawer shut, I slumped into my desk chair, tears of frustration stinging at my eyes. How could I have been such a thoughtless idiot? Cole would never forgive me, and I couldn't blame him.

Was Mixed-up Mallie back in spite of my being the Senior

Reporter and Temporary Editor?

My cell phone dinged, and I dug it out of my hobo bag. Glancing at it, I groaned as I saw Liz Ellis's name pop up. Reluctantly, I clicked on the message.

The plant killer has struck again. If you think I'm crazy, take a look at this photo.

A picture of a withered Florida leather fern was attached.

Any more deaths are going to be on your head.

Liz Ellis

Jeez. I started to flip my phone shut, but decided instead to forward the e-mail to Nick Billie with a "Plant Killer Loose on Coral Island" tag. I couldn't help a little smile as I imagined his reading Cray Cray Liz's text message.

Just then the phone on my desk rang, loud and shrill, and I jumped.

Crossing my fingers that it wasn't Liz, I reached for it. "*Observer* newsroom."

"Mallie, it's Wanda Sue. I just left a message on your cell phone: I found Bucky McGuire's body, and I'm going to be arrested for killing him. You've gotta help me!"

"What?" My head shot up. "Are you sure that Bucky is dead?"

"Tarnation, girl! I'm looking at him right now, and he's stiff as a board," she drawled, panic threaded through her voice. "What should I do? Lordy, I'm about ready to keel over myself."

I clutched the phone and tried to make sense of what my landlady was saying. "Wh-where are you?"

"At the town hall. I drove home to the Twin Palms to change into my casual outfit but had to come back here 'cause with all that ruckus, I lost one of my rhinestone earrings—you know, the ones from the Famous What's-Her-Name Movie Star Collection that I bought online a couple of weeks ago."

"Focus, Wanda Sue!"

"Sorry, hon. I can't think straight right now with this body in front of me. There. I'm turning around, so I can't see him." Her breathing came through in short, staccato bursts, as if she'd run a marathon. "Okay, that's better. Anyway, when I got here, I knew something was wrong. Things felt off; then, I realized Bucky was lying on the floor on top of the smashed-up fish tank." She swallowed audibly. "He was drenched in water with glass all around him—"

"Did he fall on the tank?"

"Not sure."

"Could he have drowned in the water after he fell over?"

"Can't tell."

"Does it look like—"

"I don't know!" she screamed. "Just get over here—pronto!"

"All right. Try to keep cool," I replied, trying to quell my own rising anxiety. "I'll call Nick Billie."

"Madame Geri already d-did," Wanda Sue stuttered.

"You called *her* first?"

"She's number one on my speed dial, and I wasn't thinking straight," she said. "It doesn't matter. She already knew about it 'cause the spirit world had told her this morning that somebody was going to die from foul play—"

"On my way." I dashed out the door, still holding the cell to my ear. "Don't say anything to Nick if he arrives before I do."

"Whadaya mean?"

Climbing into my truck, I managed not to drop the phone. "If Bucky *is* dead, and the cause *is* suspicious, you might be a . . . uh . . . under suspicion."

"But *why*?" Wanda Sue wailed.

"You found the body." I closed my eyes briefly and counted to ten for patience. "Not to mention, only a few hours ago you pointed a flare gun at Bucky during the town-hall meeting and, then, fired it at the ceiling."

"*He* was the one who said I aimed the gun at him, but it's

not true. You know that."

"Not really. I was face down on the floor, but the operative word is 'gun'." I enunciated the last word as I cranked the engine. "Got it?"

She paused, then let out a shaky exhalation. "Guess so."

"Don't touch anything. Better yet, wait outside till the paramedics and Nick arrive."

"You're a good friend, Mallie," Wanda Sue said, "especially in a crisis. You're going up to the top of my speed dial."

As I revved out of the parking lot, my confidence spiraled upward. I might've bungled my first day in charge on the job and misplaced my diamond ring, but I'd never let a friend down.

I was now *Numero Uno Mallie.*

By the time I arrived at the town-hall building, a small army had already descended on the place: emergency vehicles stood parked sideways near the entrance, and uniformed police swarmed like bees attending to an ailing hive. Red lights flashed. Sirens blared. Rushing medics barked out orders.

Total turmoil.

In the midst of it all, I noticed a tall, dark-haired man directing the activities with a sense of absolute authority: Detective Nick Billie, the island's chief detective, and one of the sexiest hunks ever. He possessed an air of command that he wore like a comfortable designer suit, and everyone looked to him for direction. His hard-planed features that bespoke his Miccosukee background remained impassive, with only a small muscle working in his cheek, betraying his inner concern.

Slowly, he turned as if sensing my presence, his black eyes piercing the distance between us. Everything and everyone melted away, and I couldn't take my eyes off him and the soulful power of a man I couldn't expel from my thoughts.

Nick.

A timeless moment passed, then I looked away for a few seconds, and he disappeared up the stairs. The sounds and the sights of the emergency scene came rushing back, along with Wanda Sue, who barreled into me, sobbing and moaning.

"Mallie, what am I going to do?" She hugged me in a desperately tight clutch that almost cut off my windpipe. I eased back a fraction and patted her giant beehive hairdo, which, miraculously, had remained intact in spite of the trauma.

"It'll be okay," I said in a soothing voice, still slightly muffled by Wanda Sue's tightening grip again. Extricating myself completely from the stranglehold, I stepped back and took stock of my landlady: tear-stained face, pinched mouth, pale skin.

Not good.

A cold knot formed in my stomach. Wanda Sue rarely lost her buoyant personality. In fact, the only time I'd actually seen her worried was when her grandson, Kevin, had disappeared, but I had found him for her and all had turned out well—sort of (that's yet another story). And the time I'd had to take her to the ER because she'd had an allergic reaction to a jar of bee cream (too many stories to count).

Otherwise, she was an upbeat, island-style, Dixie gal.

"Sorry I ain't myself." Wanda Sue sniffed, mouth trembling as she smoothed down her leopard-print tunic over skintight leggings. The Joan Rivers rhinestone earrings were back in all their dangling glory. At least Wanda Sue *looked* like herself.

"Okay, let's go through the whole story." I led her over to a white, wrought-iron settee near the front steps and sat us both down under a large, flowering jacaranda tree. Its arching branches and delicate, white flowers had a sweetly tranquil feeling, and I thought it might help to ease some of Wanda Sue's anxiety. "Start from the beginning."

After a few shaky breaths, Wanda Sue explained how she'd returned to find her earring (smart), spied the body (upsetting), and called Madame Geri (dumb).

"It was not a dumb decision to phone me," Madame Geri said, having sidled up next to me.

I clenched my jaw. How *did* she read my thoughts? "Don't you have that Joe Earl story to work on?"

"The eBay violin?" Wanda Sue's eyes widened and Madame Geri nodded. "I heard it's haunted by the image of Old Abe."

"More like some cat clawed the wood like a scratching post," I scoffed.

"I think Joe Earl has a kitten," Wanda Sue pointed out.

"Two of them." Madame Geri pulled up a decrepit wicker chair and huddled in close. "But neither of them caused the face of Abe Lincoln to appear—"

"Can we get back to what happened to Bucky McGuire?" I cut in, not even trying to disguise the annoyance in my voice. As quietly as the morning had started, this day was turning into a nightmare, and I didn't want to hear any more talk about the Great Emancipator haunting a violin when a dead body lay inside the building next to us.

Wanda Sue's mouth began to tremble again. "I found Bucky lying there next to the smashed-up fish tank. He must've fallen on it, making it tip over—the water spilling everywhere. Just an awful mess. Especially with the poor little white fish flopping around him—"

"The tilapia from the tank were still alive?" I asked, incredulous.

"Some of them," she grimaced. "When the paramedics came in, they scooped up the ones still moving and put 'em in the back kitchen sink."

"Quick thinking." I flipped open my notepad, giving Wanda Sue another reassuring pat. "Did anything seem unnatural about Bucky's death? Other than the fact that he fell on a fish tank? I mean, did he have any wounds—like he was shot or stabbed—

from what you could tell?"

Wanda Sue paused for a few moments. "I don't think so but, honey, I didn't get closer than I would to a skunk." She shuddered. "Death cooties."

"So it's possible he might've just had a stroke or heart attack and fell on the fish tank."

"He was killed." Madame Geri's blunt voice sliced through the air. She crossed her legs and folded her arms across her chest. "The vibe is off. Bucky didn't die a natural death, trust me. I told you this morning that a death was imminent."

Damn. I was hoping she'd forgotten about her possibly right-on-target prediction.

It wasn't that I trusted her so-called "spirit world" messages—not at all. But something about Bucky's demise felt off to me, too. He seemed the picture of good health only a few hours ago when he was beating Travis with a tilapia carcass—and now he was dead. Men his age didn't just bite the dust without some kind of warning.

Besides, the last two years had taught me that sudden deaths were almost *always* suspicious.

Madame Geri gave me a knowing nod that I did my best to ignore.

"It wasn't m-me that killed him," Wanda Sue stammered as she held up the flare gun. "See? It's empty. I used my last cartridge during the town-hall meeting."

"Put that thing away!" I grasped her arm and lowered it none too gently.

"What?"

"The last thing you want is for the police to see you waving a gun around right now," I hissed.

Instantly, she shoved the flare gun back in her purse. "Sorry. Mallie, I'm still freakin' out from the seeing the dead body. Bucky wasn't my . . . favorite person, but I sure didn't want to see him die like that with only stinky ole fish to buddy him off to the next world."

I shivered myself. Dying alone was one thing, but dying with only fish companions seemed worse—and bizarre.

"Wanda Sue, can I talk to you?" A deep, masculine voice wafted over to us from the doorway.

Nick Billie. I didn't even need to turn my head.

She swallowed audibly as she hauled herself upright. "I swear I didn't do anything wrong."

I took my place next to her for moral support.

"I'm not saying you did." He rested one hand on the hip of his jeans, thumb hooked around the belt loop. "But you're the one who found Bucky, so I need your statement, which I assume you've already given to Mallie." His glance moved to me. In spite of his frown, my heartbeat quickened.

"Just the barest details," I supplied, holding my landlady's elbow. "And, for the record, I came here as her friend, not as the *Observer*'s Senior Reporter."

"Admirable," he said dryly, then turned back to Wanda Sue. "Why don't we go inside? It's starting to heat up, and you can get out of the sun." He gestured with his right hand for her to follow him. "Would you like a glass of water? I know it was quite a shock for you to find Bucky."

"Oh, yes, thank you." She heaved a sigh of relief and smoothed an imaginary stray hair from her shellacked beehive. "And I didn't mean to shoot off my flare gun in the town-hall meeting. It's just that Travis and Bucky—God rest his soul—wouldn't stop fussin' at each other."

I groaned inwardly. Of course, she had to mention the flare gun first thing.

"I'd heard." Nick's mouth quirked upwards. "Probably about ten people who attended the meeting texted me pictures—and selfies."

I started to follow, but Nick pointed at the yellow crime-scene tape. "By the way, thanks for forwarding the 'plant killer' text message to my e-mail. I was out of the office, so Ms. Ellis somehow got an automatic reply from me, and she's already followed up with two e-mails."

"Trying to get you to investigate the herbicide?"

He shook his head. "She wants to file a complaint against you."

"What?" For a moment, I completely forgot about Bucky's death. "She barged into the office this morning, making all kinds of crazy statements, and then went berserk when I wouldn't do a story on her dying plants."

"She says you insulted her, and she wants to sue for damages."

"B-but that's not true . . ." My motor mouth sputtered out like a stalled engine.

"Really? Maybe you have a different idea of what defines *truth.* At any rate, I sent her the island attorney's name." With one last, ironic glance at me, he ushered Wanda Sue up the stairs.

What was he getting at? I started to follow with a protest when I spied Wanda Sue looking over her shoulder with fear-filled eyes, and I snapped back to the reality of her trauma. I gave her a little thumbs-up before they disappeared inside.

As for Nick . . . I knew he liked Wanda Sue, so I figured that he wouldn't grill her too hard. She'd just been at the wrong place at the wrong time, and Bucky's death could've been an accident anyway.

But what about that little "truth" dig Nick had tossed at me? Was he referring to Liz, or something else? Did he know I was engaged to Cole and had neglected to tell him?

A ridiculous thought. Still . . . a small twinge of excitement tugged at me, causing my cheeks to grow flushed.

Fanning myself, I slid back onto the settee and recalled with a stern inner voice that Nick had never actually *said* how he felt about me—ever.

I'm a journalist; I need to hear the words.

"Nick loves you," Madame Geri spoke up, reading my thoughts yet again. But this time, it probably wasn't any of her psychic messages or my panicked doodles; my red face betrayed my inner musings.

"I don't want to talk about it. I'm engaged to Cole," I replied in a firm voice. "And we've got bigger issues right now than my chaotic love life." I pointed at the medics carrying emergency equipment out of the building without haste. "I guess there's no need to rush now Bucky is . . . gone."

"He's crossed over," Madame Geri said in a sober tone, "on a different kind of journey."

"One he wasn't expecting," I added.

"No."

"You can't hide from fate, and you can't hide from your true feelings." Madame Geri pursed her mouth as she sat back on the wicker chair, her elbows propped up on the arm rests. "They have a way of coming out when you least expect them."

I sighed. She wouldn't give up on her new-age psychoanalysis until we had an in-depth girl talk about my future. "I don't know *what* I feel. Cole and Nick are 'enigmas wrapped in riddles,' and I can't seem to figure out which one of them is the man of my dreams. Or at least the guy most likely to live happily ever after with my fast-food/coffee addiction."

"Hmm." She tapped her chin. "Has it ever occurred to you that *you're* the 'enigma,' and the men in your life are trying to figure you out?"

"But . . . nothing is hidden about me. I put everything out there, mainly 'cause I don't have the ability to keep secrets—from anybody. You know my story: I have an Airstream at the

Twin Palms RV Park, my doggy companion is a teacup poodle named Kong . . . oh, and don't forget I have a geriatric handyman with a crush on me—mainly because I have an unerring way of finding his dentures. End of the Fascinating Mallie Monroe Life History. Book closed—*finis.*"

"More like *in medias res.*" She smiled. "In the midst of things."

"Drop it, will you?" I stopped fanning myself. "I have to help Wanda Sue right now. She just found a dead body and is being questioned by our island cop probably as a 'person of interest.' If there's something suspicious about Bucky's death, she could be a suspect down the road."

"She didn't do it. We both know that." Madame Geri gazed out across the island foliage, and I followed her glance over to the thick growth of saw palmetto and cabbage palm trees, peppered with creeping sea-grape vines. Coral Island had a rural feel to it, with large open spaces of untouched tropical vegetation. They made the island seem bigger than it was—and feel emptier when the snowbird tourists flew north. It would seem *really* empty if Wanda Sue weren't around.

"For once, I agree with you. Wanda Sue is a total cream puff about hurting people, animals, plants, anything. We have to force her to use pest control at the Twin Palms so our trailers and RVs aren't overrun with palmetto bugs."

"Bugs have to live, too."

Uh-huh. "I don't suppose Bucky has given you a hint as to what happened to him?" Call me desperate, but I was willing to give the spiritual grapevine a try if it meant I could help Wanda Sue.

"It's not like a telephone call," Madame Geri said dryly. Still, she closed her eyes briefly. "All I'm getting is 'water,' from Bucky."

I shot her a twisted smile. "Big surprise there since he died in a fish tank."

"Sometimes spirits don't know what happened to them."

"The Great Beyond is fascinating, but I need to get a plan to help Wanda Sue."

Madame Geri focused her gaze back on me. "What should we do about it?"

"There's no 'we.' Wanda Sue called *me*—"

"She called me, too—"

"But this is *my* story; you've got that dead-president-on-a-violin headline to work on. Let's not put that *Dummy's Guide* to waste. Remember?" I held my hands in front of me, as if reading an imaginary book. "You promised to help me out at the *Observer* this week."

She clamped her mouth into a tight line.

"Madame Geri, *please* let me handle this one. Wanda Sue is my best friend on the island, and I want to be there for her like she has been for me. When I drove onto Coral Island two years ago with fifty bucks in my purse, ready to start my new job at the newspaper, Wanda Sue let me park my Airstream at the Twin Palms for free until I had my first paycheck. She has a big heart to match her big hair, and I wouldn't have survived without her." *Damn skippy.* "Besides, I'm going to need the violin story since Bernice's bicycle bandit isn't likely to be much of anything."

"Well, tip number two in the *Dummy's Guide* says to go with 'your gut,' and the Old Abe apparition is almost guaranteed Pulitzer Prize material." She gave a quick nod of her head. "It's probably best that I put my energy there, but you'll need help on the Bucky McGuire story. Ask Bernice."

"I can handle it."

Wanda Sue stumbled down the town-hall steps. "My life is over. I'm going to jail!"

Maybe I spoke too soon.

Chapter Four

I rushed over to steady Wanda Sue as she reached the bottom step.

"I'm going to the slammer. The big house." Her eyes widened in desperation as she grasped my shoulders. "But I can't go to jail! I have a daughter and a grandson. Who would look after Kevin if his granny was a jailbird?"

"You're not going to prison." I tried to reassure her as I pried her clawing fingers from around my collarbones.

She gulped. "I . . . I . . ."

While she struggled for words, I steered her in the direction of the settee again. She collapsed and dropped her head in her hands.

"What happened in there?"

"Nothing happened," Nick Billie said in an even voice as he strolled toward us. "I took Wanda Sue's statement and then told her if she fired off a flare gun again, I would put her in jail for disturbing the peace."

"See?" Wanda Sue's head came up again. "Jail!"

"It was only a w-a-r-n-i-n-g." I spelled out the word, enunciating each consonant and vowel. "I agree with Nick. You shouldn't even be carrying a flare gun in your bag."

Wanda Sue nodded mutely, retrieved the gun from her purse, and handed it over to Nick.

"We haven't established that there is anything irregular about Bucky's death yet," Nick continued, glancing down at Wanda

Sue with a mixture of kindness and amusement. "Your statement was to give facts *only* about how you found the body and what you did after that."

Wanda Sue tugged on his shirtsleeve. "You mean I'm not going to be on a chain gang?"

"Hardly." Nick's mouth twitched, as he tried to keep a solemn expression intact while patting her hand. "You haven't been accused of anything in Bucky's death."

"Thank the good Lord, 'cause I could never wear one of those funny orange jumpsuits that make you look like a turnip in a sack." Wanda Sue visibly shuddered as she released Nick's arm. "You know, I pride myself on having a Dixie-gal fashionista sense."

"You could be on the cover of *Southern Belle* magazine." I crossed my fingers behind my back to ward off bad juju at the lie.

She managed a tremulous smile and started to heave herself off the wicker settee. But as she straightened, her legs began to quake, and she slipped down again. Quick to notice, Nick steadied her descent with a firm grasp on her elbow.

"Take it easy, Wanda Sue," he said.

"Oh, my. All of this uproar has taken more out of me than I realized." Her breathing became labored, causing her chest to heave in and out like a massive balloon inflating and deflating. "I feel like I'm going to faint."

"Paramedic, over here!" Nick shouted as he motioned over a young man who was walking toward the emergency vehicles, pushing an oxygen tank.

"Yes, sir." Instantly, he was at Wanda Sue's side, checking her pulse and heart rate. "Your beat is a little rapid, ma'am, but your heart sounds fine. Just sit still for a few minutes while I check your blood pressure."

Wanda Sue sat quietly, taking in a few deep breaths as he

cuffed her with the blood pressure strap. Eventually, her legs stopped shaking and her chest calmed to a steady rhythm.

"I . . . I'm okay now." She exhaled in another long, audible breath. "I must have hyperventriculated from the fuss."

The medic looked at me, and I silently mouthed, "hyperventilated."

He nodded as he peeled off the strap. "Your blood pressure is normal, but I don't think you should drive, ma'am. Is there someone who could take you home?"

Wanda Sue waved a hand in dissent. "Oh, I don't think I need that. Besides, my car—"

"I'll drive her home." Madame Geri's voice was firm, final, and none of us protested. After some complicated group maneuvers to get Wanda Sue upright and settled into Madame Geri's old-style Volvo, I waved them off. Then I suddenly became very aware that I'd been left alone with Nick Billie.

I looked down at my Birkenstocks and kicked a shell fragment that had been crushed into the grass. It flew all of about six inches. Then I toed another one that went a bit farther, trying to think of something to say.

Nothing witty, clever, or even mildly droll came to me. My motor mouth was stuck in neutral—and the hushed quiet stretched between us like silent chain lightning, jagged and electric.

I cleared my throat and finally mumbled something about the unpredictable weather.

"They're finishing up inside," Nick said, ignoring my pathetic attempts at chitchat. "You know, I went easy on Wanda Sue when I took her statement, but I had to warn her about the flare gun. It's protocol."

"I know." Looking up, I still avoided his eyes, searching around for a neutral comment that wouldn't dig my landlady in any deeper. "Just for the record, she wasn't the only one who was acting like an idiot during that meeting. All of the town-council candidates took part in the screaming match, especially after the fish handout began—"

"That had to be Bucky," he interjected.

" 'Fraid so. He had a whole cooler full of tilapia in his truck, I guess, and saw them as his ticket to being a shoo-in for town council."

"People have leveraged political success on less. I heard that he and Travis went at it pretty hard."

"That's an understatement." I gave a short laugh, then grew serious again as I thought of Bucky's body inside the town hall. "Granted, Bucky acted like a complete jackass, but he seemed awfully healthy to die so . . . suddenly." I paused. "Do you think someone—"

"Killed him in the tilapia tank?"

I nodded, waiting for Nick to berate me for hinting at foul play, as per Madame Geri's suspicion, and I couldn't say I'd blame him. It was way too soon to even speculate.

"I don't know. It's possible."

"Huh?" I did a double take at his unexpected response. "Wait a minute. You're not irritated that I suggested someone might've murdered Bucky before you've even done an autopsy?" Had I entered a bizarro world?

Now it was his turn to give a short laugh. "Even I have to admit the circumstances of his death are . . . unusual."

"And?" I prompted. He knew something.

"There were signs . . . of blunt trauma to the back of Bucky's head."

"Could the fall have caused the wound?"

Nick shook his head. "It looks like he went down face first."

"Okay. Not likely." I tried to imagine various scenarios about how Bucky could've taken a konk to the back of the head. It didn't take me more than a few moments to rule out almost everything but a deliberate attack. "If someone did kill Bucky, you've got plenty of suspects from the town-hall meeting—except Wanda Sue, of course."

He didn't respond.

"I thought she was off the hook." I chewed my lower lip as anxiety spurted through me.

"She is . . . for now." Nick frowned and raked a hand through his dark hair. "You probably don't know this, but Wanda Sue dated Bucky a few years ago, even though he's a good ten years younger—"

"What?"

"It happened before you came to Coral Island. They had a bad breakup, and Bucky said Wanda Sue had tried to attack him with a frying pan."

"She never cooks," I protested.

"Maybe not, but he filed a complaint nevertheless," Nick countered. "Later, Bucky started seeing a woman who lives in Paradisio, and things blew over. But all of that history means she might have a motive to turn violent on him. At the time, I had to take Bucky's complaint seriously, no matter how out of character his allegations seemed for Wanda Sue."

We fell silent again.

"Speaking of couples," Nick finally spoke up, "when are you and Cole going to get married?"

My attention immediately snapped back to Nick.

"So you know about my engagement?"

"Yep."

I was tempted to avoid the conversation and return to my shell kicking, but that wouldn't help things much. "Look, I've known Cole for a long time. We lived together in Orlando before he took off to find himself in the wilds of New Mexico. When he showed up here last summer, we decided to be . . . friends. But, then, he asked me to marry him two weeks ago, and I sort of said 'yes.' "

"Sort of?"

I met his glance squarely. "I'm thirty and not getting any younger."

"What about you and me?"

My heart fluttered. "*Is* there a 'you and me'?"

"I thought we were edging there, until I showed up at your trailer, and you were two-timing me with Cole. No. Three-timing me, if you count Pop Pop." A ghost of a smile touched his face.

"I don't count Pop Pop. Besides, it wasn't like you and I had a thing going," I said, feeling the waves of heat rise to my face. Okay, I confess: I'd planned dinner dates with both Cole and Nick. But hadn't I been punished enough by having to eat dinner with Pop Pop, while watching him drop his dentures into a water glass? "You're busy with your job twenty-four-seven and, if you come up for air, it's usually to gripe at me for interfering with an investigation."

"All true." He moved closer and lifted a lock of my red hair; he twisted it around his finger. "But you have to admit that you, too, can be maddening."

I put my hand over his. "Maybe we're just not meant to be together."

"Do you really believe that?" Nick's voice deepened. Then he grasped my palm and moved it to his mouth. He placed a kiss in the soft spot beneath my thumb, and my pulse skittered.

"I . . . I don't know." Attraction radiated to all parts of my body, and I barely restrained myself from embracing him with every ounce of my rising passion. *Hot, hot, hot.*

He slowly propelled me toward him.

As my arms slid around his neck, my chin tilted up, and I could already feel his lips on mine. Then, an image of Cole rose up in my mind, and I froze. "No."

I pulled back, steeling myself to the surge of desire that had stirred all of my senses. "I can't. Not when I'm engaged to another man."

"I don't see an engagement ring."

"Uh . . . I don't need a piece of jewelry to remind me that I have a fiancé." That was true. I just left off the part about misplacing the diamond. "I love Cole."

Nick stared down at me for a few seconds, then pivoted on his heel, not looking back as he walked away. The gravel crunched under his shoes with a hard, grinding sound.

I began to stop him but, instead, let him go.

It was over.

After watching Nick drive off, I climbed into Rusty and headed back to the *Observer* with a heavy heart. How could I have gotten myself into this situation? I was engaged to Cole—my buddy that I liked more than French fries—but I longed for Nick, the man I wanted more than a Krispy Kreme donut.

Obviously, they both rated high on my junk-food meter.

Maybe I just needed to date a food coach from Weight Watchers and be done with both of them.

Or maybe Bucky's death had scrambled all ability to think straight, whether I scarfed down fast food or not.

My emotions still in turmoil, I finally turned into the newspaper's parking lot and gave myself a mental shake. This relationship angst was tearing me up, and I needed all of my focus to get out this week's edition. The "election antics" story had amped up into a potential piece on an untimely death—and maybe more. Closing my eyes while I sat in my battered, rust-ridden truck for a few moments, I tried to regain my equilibrium. But images of Nick and Cole flitted through my mind: the night Nick kissed me outside the Taste of Venice restaurant; the day Cole asked me to marry him under my Airstream awning. Hard to say which one excited me more.

A tap on the window startled me, and my eyes flew open.

"Look what Joe Earl brought in!" Madame Geri stood there, brandishing a battered old violin. "After looking at the real deal, there's not a chance in hell you can say this isn't Abe Lincoln." She traced the swirling lines etched near the chin rest. "See?"

Shoving all thoughts of the men in my life out of my mind, I threw open the door and climbed out, striding past Madame Geri as I murmured, "I don't need to look at it; what a piece of phony baloney."

"You can run, but you can't hide from the truth," she said, following me into the *Observer* office. "This violin is practically a portal to communicating with Old Abe himself."

"Really? Tell him the stovepipe hat was a big mistake." I tossed her a glance over my shoulder. "How was Wanda Sue by the time you got her home?"

"Still upset." Madame Geri kept on my heels. "But hanging in there."

"Okay. Thanks." I halted as I spied a twenty-something geek of a guy sitting at my desk, clicking away on his iPhone. He wore one of those splashy, Florida graphic t-shirts complemented by short, sun-bleached hair gelled into spiky points.

"I'm Joe Earl." He waved the phone in my direction.

"Hi." I waved back as I moved toward him. "I think you're sitting at my desk."

"Really? It's a cool spot." He thumped the ancient wooden desk, causing it to shake on its aging legs. Then he resumed texting on his iPhone as he put his flip-flop clad feet on my desk.

I circled around him and opened the drawer to check on my engagement ring. *Damn.* No diamond. No hope.

Sighing in frustration, I threw my hobo bag on Sandy's desk, realizing this was going to be *my* temporary new "cool spot" since I couldn't stand to sit in Anita's pigsty of an office—more bad juju.

At least the main office didn't have that empty, deserted feeling anymore. It was downright bustling, with several stories in the hopper, including another potential murder case. Granted, I could've done without Marley perched on my file cabinet as he surveyed the entire scene. His black wings lay flat, but his head swiveled incessantly, keeping tabs on every person's movements—especially mine.

At that moment, it got a lot busier as Bernice pedaled a bicycle out of Anita's office, ringing the bell on the handlebars. She'd traded her miniskirt for leather pants, but still wore the wig. "Hey, the bicycle thief left this gem at the Circle-K. Wahoo! I haven't been on a bike in ages, but I guess the old saying is right about how it comes back to you. Outta my way!" She rang the bell again as she mowed down a trash can and aimed for the front door.

But Madame Geri had just entered the office in my wake and stood rooted near the doorway, her arms wrapped around the violin in a protective embrace.

Bernice tried to wheel around her by jerking the handlebars with a hard left, but Madame Geri moved in the same direction, trying to get out of the way. Bernice turned in the opposite direction and rammed into the doorjamb. The impact caused her to flip over, hitting the floor with a crash and some loud cursing.

Marley squawked loudly and began to flap his wings.

My breath caught in my throat.

"I think I broke my collarbone. Dammit," Bernice exclaimed. "Someone help me."

The parrot's squawking grew more piercing, and I covered my ears. "Madame Geri, calm down your bird."

Joe Earl reached back and stroked the parrot's feathers, calming him down.

"Marley likes you?" I asked in amazement as my hands fell away from my head.

He nodded.

"Bernice, you're a dimwitted fool," Madame Geri berated her, cradling the violin. "If this violin had been damaged, you would've destroyed a piece of spiritual history. Do you understand that? It would be almost a sacrilege against one of our most beloved presidents."

Bernice waved off the question as she edged out from under that bicycle. "Don't everybody help me at once."

"Okay." I pulled out my cell phone. Joe Earl was still occupied with calming down Marley.

Bernice struggled to her feet, rubbing her hipbone and glaring at Madame Geri. "I told you to get outta my way. Now a crucial piece of evidence in the bicycle thief investigation could be ruined."

"That's small potatoes compared to Joe Earl's psychic violin."

"Says you." Bernice righted the bicycle, but the front spokes had bent in the crash, causing the whole tire to tilt off-kilter. She tried to hop on again, but the seat fell off as she swung her leg over it. "Great, just great."

Madame Geri carefully set the violin on my purloined desk in front of Joe Earl with solemn reverence. "The whole bicycle-thief thing is a tidal bore, not a front-page story by any stretch of the imagination."

"This bike is evidence." Bernice muttered more curses under her breath as she tried to fasten the seat back on. "It's part of my *headline* story."

"Neither of these pieces is much more than a sidebar," I said, resisting the urge to kick the bicycle and toss the violin out the door. "Bucky McGuire just died at the town-hall building, surrounded by nothing but flopping tilapia. That's our main story, especially if he were *murdered.*"

The last word finally caused Joe Earl to cease his parrot pacification. "Somebody killed that dude with the bad comb-over?"

"Maybe." I sat in Sandy's chair, pulled out my notepad, and began flipping through the pages. "We won't know till Nick Billie has the autopsy report to show cause of death. In the meantime, we have to cover the story as an unexplained death." At least as the temporary editor, I *sounded* like I knew what I was talking about.

"I *guess* that might trump my story," Bernice admitted grudgingly as she rubbed her shoulder. "But time is of the essence to find out if it was foul play."

"No need to wait," Madame Geri said. "I can try to contact the spirit world about Bucky again, but this time with a more open channel."

All three of us sucked in our collective breaths.

She pointed at the violin.

"Oh, no." I raised both hands in dissent. "We are *not* going to rely on a musical instrument to tell us whether a killer is on the loose on the island again."

"Wow." Joe Earl lowered his feet and whistled under his breath. "Is it going to . . . like, *speak* to us? I knew the violin was special, but this just blows my mind."

"Maybe it could sing show tunes." Bernice threw the bike down and limped over to my desk as Joe Earl gave up my chair to Madame Geri.

"Don't be ridiculous," Madame Geri responded, setting the violin on my desk so that it stretched out horizontally in front of her. "It will vibrate its answers." She placed both palms on the chin rest.

"Like a psychic tuning fork?" I scoffed.

Ignoring me, she placed one hand on the violin's chin rest

and the other on its neck. "Was Bucky McGuire killed?"

Bernice and Joe Earl leaned over the desk; and, in spite of my now possessing the status of Senior Reporter and Temporary Editor, I did the same. Two years of chasing down leads, verifying sources, and checking public records for legitimate newspaper stories had boiled down to watching an image of Abe Lincoln on a violin for a headline.

Chapter Five

I held my breath. If Madame Geri were right about this one, I'd eat my Miami Dolphins cap Cole had given me—not a great sacrifice since I hated football anyway.

"I feel something," she said, closing her eyes as her fingers skimmed along the instrument. "The violin is about to answer the question of 'Who killed Bucky McGuire?'."

"Cripes, you've already asked that question. You're leading the 'witness' like a psycho CSI agent," Bernice pronounced in disgust.

Madame Geri raised a brow. "Psychic."

"Whatever." Bernice pulled up a chair as she kept massaging her shoulder. "No one seems to care that I may need surgery after that wipeout on the bike."

"You're too ornery to break anything. It's probably just a bruise," I quipped. Not to mention, Bernice had quite a bit of padding on her upper arms that would cushion any hard-floor landing.

"Get a Reiki massage. It'll release any toxins from the fall," Madame Geri added.

Joe Earl tapped something on his iPhone screen. "I've got an app for that."

"Okay, I can't stand here all afternoon, waiting for this stupid violin to give us a message."

Madame Geri cast a warning glance in my direction. "I'm starting to receive something from the next world." The violin moved slightly on my desk.

"*You're* doing that!" Bernice sneered as she folded her arms across her chest. "This is bogus."

"I'm not touching it anymore." Madame Geri wiggled her fingers, so we could tell they were above the violin.

"Cool." Joe Earl snapped a picture.

The violin paused, then slowly slid across the desk with a whisper of its mahogany finish against cheap, pressed wood. All the while Madame Geri's hands hovered above it. In spite of my skepticism that she was somehow really moving it, my eyes were riveted on the violin. It skimmed along, stopping and starting a couple of times, finally halting with the neck across one of Sandy's magazines, *Today's Bride*. "There's your answer." Madame Geri tapped the cover.

"*What?*" Bernice snatched up the periodical. "What does a picture of some young chippy in a wedding dress standing near a pond have to do with murder? Spare me." Bernice tossed the magazine at me. "I'm getting back to my *real* news story on the 'bicycle bandit.' After I stop at the drugstore and pick up some Ben-Gay." She clumped out of the office, giving the bike a little kick en route.

"Oh, ye of little faith." Madame Geri patted the violin. "It gave us its message. You just have to figure it out. Tip number three in the *Dummy's Guide* is 'Don't rule out the unlikely.' "

"Hey, maybe the violin was played at a wedding when someone was killed," Joe Earl offered.

"How would that relate to Bucky's death?" Intrigued in spite of myself, I picked up the magazine and scanned the other cover stories: caterer tips (yawn), invitation card suggestions (doze), and honeymoon tips (yikes). Nothing of much use there. "Your psychic world must be out for dinner, which is where I'm going to be in"—I checked my Mickey Mouse watch—"another half hour."

"Take the magazine with you." Madame Geri held it out to me. "You might need it."

"For my upcoming wedding?"

"No, for the murder investigation," she corrected me, flipping the pages of the magazine. "The violin has spoken."

"You keep it," I urged with a wave of my hand. "I like my journalism the old-fashioned way: legwork and snooping. In fact, I would swing by Bucky's house on my way home—if I knew where he lived—just to check things out. That's what a *real* reporter does when she's trying to get the facts, not interrogate a violin."

Raising my chin, I started for the door.

"His house is at 572 Seaside Lane near the Blue Creek Marina. It's about seven minutes from here." Joe Earl held up his iPhone with a grin.

I gave him a curt nod of thanks. "Of course, the 'legwork' includes technology," I added.

Madame Geri tipped her fedora.

"Would you mind if I asked the violin a couple of questions?" Joe Earl turned back to her. "I lost my friend's iPod yesterday and maybe the violin could give me a few pointers on where to look."

"Of course you may," she responded with a smile to Joe Earl. "There are no dumb questions—just dumb disbelievers." The last words were uttered in my direction, so I grabbed my hobo bag and headed for the door before I could hear any more of this psychic mumbo jumbo.

Cole and I were going to have a nice dinner and enjoy some couple time. Just what I needed to dispel my doubts.

I paused, the image of my fiancé rising up in my mind. Could it be that the violin might actually help me find my lost engagement ring?

I glanced back at the two of them and saw Joe Earl's spiked

hair and Madame Geri's felt fedora both bent over the violin with eager intent as Marley watched the whole proceedings from his perch. I hesitated. Then a brisk wind pulled the door open, and I felt a blast of coolness through my thin, cotton sweater.

Time to go home, after I swung by Bucky's house.

I hopped into Rusty, started the engine, and headed north on Cypress Drive. Seaside Lane was the last turn on the right before the road curved left along the shoreline toward the Twin Palms RV Resort, my home.

After making the turn, I checked the mailboxes for Bucky's address. Once I found it, I turned Rusty into the driveway and scanned the property. It was a typical three/two, one-story, stuccoed house with a pool and canal in the backyard. Nothing special, except for the lush vegetation. Bucky might've been a fish-thumping good ole boy, but he knew his landscaping. Huge royal palms lined the driveway, hibiscus bushes bloomed everywhere with their scarlet flowers, and sea-grape vines adorned the archway that led to the front door.

The entire front lawn teemed with life like a tropical paradise—sadly. But who would take care of the yard now that Bucky was dead? I gulped, not wanting to allow my thoughts to go there. It was too raw. Too painful.

I scanned the rest of the yard, but nothing looked amiss. Just to make sure, I slid out of Rusty and moved toward the front of the house. After tripping over a garden hose, I made it to the front windows and peered inside. Everything looked neat and orderly. No one had gone in to trash the place. In fact, I cast an admiring glance at the brown leather furniture. Granted, it was a "man-colored" sectional sofa, but it looked snug and inviting compared to my crummy couch.

Just as I was imagining myself melting into the soft leather, I felt a hard tap on my shoulder.

I shrieked and stepped back, ready to run for my truck.

"Hey, I didn't mean to startle you, but what are you doing here?" a middle-aged man said in a quiet voice. "This is Bucky McGuire's house." He held a machete in his right hand.

"I . . . I . . ." I swallowed hard, eying the sharp blade. *Keep it together.* "I'm Mallie Monroe, Senior Reporter for the *Observer.* I met Bucky today at the town-hall meeting, so I guess I qualify as a friend. Well, maybe that's too strong—an acquaintance, perhaps? Anyway, I just wanted to see what his house looked like because he mentioned his landscaping business earlier today, and I thought I might like to . . . uh, use his company's services to fix up the area around my Airstream . . ." *Liar, liar.* Next, I'll be growing a Pinocchio nose and Anita-style chin hair. *No, I wouldn't go there.* "Okay, to tell you the truth—"

"Bucky's dead and you wanted to check his place out?" He raked a hand through his silver hair. He wore it long, pulled back into a small ponytail, with a doo-rag around his scalp and forehead.

"Unfortunately, yes to both questions."

His eyes filled with tears as he dropped the machete.

"Did you know him?" I nudged the machete handle off to the side, out of his reach.

"He was my boss." The man's head dropped to his grass-stained shirt for a few moments as his shoulders heaved with emotion. Then he looked up again, his eyes dimmed with the shadow of grief. "He gave me a job when no one else on the island would take a chance on me. It's a terrible thing when you want to work, earn your keep, but people think your medical condition will keep you from doing the job." He thumped his right leg, then bent and flexed it.

"Bum knee?" I asked.

"No short-term memory." He shook his head with a sigh.

Yikes.

"It makes it kinda hard to be a top-notch worker when I don't remember details too well. But Bucky and I had a system; he'd write down all the jobs that I had to do and then pin them on my pocket." He pointed at a small piece of paper attached to his shirt. "See, right here: 'Trim bushes in Bucky's front yard.' That's what I was doing."

I squinted to read the small handwriting. Sure enough, that's what it said.

"It doesn't seem all that different from what my boss, Anita, does, except she sends my assignments through the computer," I pointed out. I still had most of my memory, but the "pin method" might not be a bad thing for Bernice since she had the occasional senior moment.

He held out his hand. "By the way, I'm Cooper Naylor, but everyone calls me Coop."

"Hi, Coop." We shook hands. "So, how are you holding up overall?"

"I'm still standing, but I've had some bad moments this afternoon. I mean, I can hardly believe it that Bucky keeled over on a fish tank—that's what they were saying at the Island Hardware store. Just yesterday, he was working a tough job with me—planting and trimming for one of our nursery clients. We worked the whole day, and he wasn't even breathing hard. Jeez."

"So, he didn't have any health problems?"

"Nope. And I know for a fact that he got a physical every year—we both did—'cause you have to pass a certification test to run heavy equipment." He frowned. "At least I think we did."

"Sounds plausible." Best to keep to myself that Detective Billie already suspected foul play.

"I keep all of the notes that Bucky pinned to my shirt. If I could just remember where I put them."

"The police can always check state records about the

certification." I looked at the house again; it already felt empty. "Did Bucky have any . . . enemies?"

His face shuttered down and his eyes narrowed. "What do you mean?"

Shifting my weight from one foot to the other, I cleared my throat. "If Bucky's death turns out to be suspicious, it might be helpful to know if anyone had it in for him."

"I told you that he was a great boss." Coop's mouth set in a stubborn line.

"Of course, but I saw at least one person today at the town-council meeting who didn't care for Bucky—"

"Travis?"

"Uh-huh."

"He's just plain scum, and I'll tell anyone that who wants to hear it." Coop's voice kindled with anger. "He didn't treat Bucky right, and a lot of islanders know that aside from me."

"What exactly did Travis do?"

"I can't talk about this anymore," he cut in. "It just isn't the time, and I need to get a hold of myself and figure out what I'm supposed to do with Bucky's business."

"Did he have any children?"

"No kids. No brothers or sisters—that I remember."

"So, it's up to you to keep the biz going?"

"Miss whatever-your-name-is, you're trespassing, so I'm going to have to ask you to move along." He gestured toward my truck with a shaky hand. Tears spilled down his sun-weathered cheeks in tiny rivulets, colorless as pure water.

Instantly, I felt sort of guilty about pressing him for information. He was right; it wasn't the time. "Look, if you want to talk with me again, I'm going to give you my card. It has my e-mail address and phone number." I slipped it into his pocket. "Will you remember?"

He patted his shirt. "Yep. I always check my pockets."

"Thanks, Coop, and I'm sorry for your loss." I meant it. I started to leave, but he looked so forlorn just standing there, I turned and hugged him. "Take care."

He gave a brief nod and bit his lip.

As I pulled up to my little corner of paradise ten minutes later, I parked my truck under the blue and white awning of my gleaming, silver Airstream. *Aah.* A symbol of freedom in its hut-like sturdiness, it was truly home, sweet home. And a haven away from the trauma of Bucky's death, Wanda Sue's interrogation, and Coop's grief.

It had been one hell-on-wheels type of day.

The sun had already set and darkness was creeping in.

As I jumped out of Rusty and hurried toward the warmth of my trailer, I noticed the fifth-wheeler parked next door seemed unnaturally quiet. No activity emanated from any window. Of course, the temperature had started dropping, so maybe my new neighbor was hunkered down for the evening.

Cole's van, on the other side of my site, also showed no sign of life. Good. I could make a nice dinner (order a pizza and salad) and break the news about Bucky's death and misplaced engagement ring—in that order—hoping the day's trauma at the town hall might distract him from the lost diamond. I winced even as I articulated the cruddy plan to myself, but I was desperate.

As I swung open my Airstream door, Kong did his usual flying leap at me, and I enjoyed a few moments of doggy love before I grabbed his leather leash and headed him to the beach for the second time today. On the way, I took another peep through the darkness at my mystery neighbor's fifth-wheel trailer; there was still no sign of activity, except the chili-pepper lights were on, and a toy flamingo played Spanish guitar on top the picnic table to the Latin tune "If You Had My Love."

Could J-Lo be next door? She owned a house in Miami, if the gossip mags were right.

I made a mental note to pump Wanda Sue for information.

After Kong had completed his task, I hustled him back into the Airstream and proceeded to beautify myself for the upcoming "truth and consequences" talk with Cole. But as I showered and slapped on a little makeup, my thoughts keep drifting back to the Bucky part of my day. Then I flashed back to Coop's heartfelt reaction and guilt rose up inside me like bile. I couldn't just use his death to divert Cole; it was wrong. Better to "fess up"—as Wanda Sue would say—and take the consequences.

Bucky's demise had to be respected.

Finishing up with my Peachy Keen lipstick, a thought suddenly popped into my head: how could a killer have sneaked up behind Bucky to administer the death blow without Bucky noticing and turning around? The town-hall building had a tiled floor, so the killer's footsteps would've been audible.

I stared at my own freckled face, looking for an answer—and I had it: Bucky must've known his murderer. The killer had lured him into feeling comfortable. Then, when Bucky turned toward the fish tank, the killer struck with a blow that came down hard on the back of his head. Bucky then went face down in the tilapia tank, causing it to tip over and shatter.

Dollars to donuts, that's how he died.

But who did it?

All I knew was that it could not have been Wanda Sue.

I sighed, focusing once more on the image in the mirror with a critical eye. Black dress (bought from Secondhand Rose thrift store), freckled arms and freckled legs (a curse), and thick, scarlet curls (a blessing—and my best feature, hands down). Not bad, especially since my thin, albeit rather flat-chested, body was hidden by the drapy material.

I put on another layer of Peachy Keen.

Maybe getting married would be the best thing for me. I could stick just to *writing* about murders and not investigating them, which had proven to be bad for my health in the past. A husband wouldn't want me to spend my nights chasing down criminals and putting myself in harm's way.

Except that I wouldn't see Nick nearly as often.

And I wouldn't be doing something that I loved.

Maybe getting married would be the worst thing for me.

A wave of distress overcame me. So, I was right back at square one in a total quandary about whether I wanted to get married or not.

How could I still be having those thoughts when I was engaged to Cole?

Come on, girl. Get it together.

Just then my cell phone dinged.

I picked it up—and almost threw it down again. Liz Ellis.

Sighing, I flipped it open.

The plant killer has struck yet again. I guess the picture of the leather fern wasn't enough to convince you; take a look at my areca palms. I lost ten of them today.

I scanned the picture. So the palm trees had shriveled, brown fronds? How was that a front-page story?

When is it going to be enough for you to take action?

I've already contacted the police and reported the crimes and, unlike you, the detective I spoke to was well-mannered and civil.

Call me if you want to make amends.

Liz Ellis.

P.S. I've contacted the island attorney and intend to sue you for journalistic discrimination.

Cray Cray Liz strikes again.

As I contemplated answering her, a loud knock on my door caused me to raise my head. I checked the clock: 6:30 p.m.

Cole? Early?

Kong began to yap excitedly with a shrill, happy bark of recognition. I headed through the Airstream and swung open the door—to behold Wanda Sue, who stood there in a neon yellow warm-up suit that almost exactly matched her canary-colored hair. She carried a pair of orange coveralls draped over her arm and wore cork-heeled wedgie sandals.

"Brrrrrrr, hon! The thermostat is dropping, and I'm colder than a dead pig in the sunshine." She rubbed her hands together and stamped her wedgies on the ground as she shifted from foot to foot to stay warm. "Aren't you gonna get me out of the wind?"

"Uh . . . sure. I'm sorry." I'd been mesmerized for the hundredth time by the ability of her massive beehive hair to stay intact, in spite of a gale-force wind. She must use liquid cement to achieve that kind of sturdy bouffant.

She hurried in, and took a seat on my sofa very near the furnace vent. After a few moments of taking in the warmth, she visibly relaxed. "Honey, I've spent my life here and in North Florida, and I can tell ya, it's true that your blood thins. Mine is probably like water by now."

"I feel it, too, and I've only been a couple of years on Coral Island," I agreed, seating myself across from her in an armchair. "How about a cup of coffee?"

"Manna from heaven, girl." She grinned. "You look prettier than a glob of butter on a stack of pancakes."

"Thanks." *High praise indeed.* In five steps, I was in the kitchen area, reaching for the coffee pot. One of the many things I loved about my Airstream was that it was so compact—no spot in my funky home-on-wheels took more than a dozen steps to get to. I could eat a pizza and, in two bites, be situated in the bedroom watching television and, by the time I munched on the crust, be back in the kitchen for another slice. I was like the old woman who lived in the shoe—minus the kids.

Who could argue with that type of easy living?

Maybe a husband.

"Are you and Cole gonna buy a house once you're married?" Wanda Sue asked.

I dropped the coffee scoop, spilling my Island Java all over the counter in a smattering of smoky granules. "I have a home. My Airstream." I brushed the coffee to the edge of the counter and carefully nudged it back into the scooper. No need to waste good, unused grounds.

As I tipped the scoop into the filter and filled the pot with water, my mind began to race. Would I have to sell my Airstream when Cole and I were wed? How could I? This sleek, silver abode was my dream place; I'd lovingly restored it from the bottom up. And it was . . . well, perfect.

"Life changes when you get married, honey." Wanda Sue's eyes met mine as I moved back into the living area—hers full of gentle understanding. "Guess you didn't think about that part. Most people don't. But your whole world will be turned upside down with a new hubby. I loved being married, don't get me wrong, but living with my dear, departed hubby required some adjustments." She leaned back on the sofa, her face taking on an expression of reverie—glazed eyes and soft smile. "He was up at dawn; I'm a late riser. He liked cats; I'm a dog lover. He liked the mountains; I liked the beach."

"Okay, I get the picture," I cut in with some alarm. "But Cole and I have lived together before; we spent a couple of years in Orlando in this Airstream."

"But you weren't married. That puts a different spin on everything."

My racing thoughts amped up to a mental marathon of panic. *Don't go there.* I could not allow myself to go there. "I'll get the coffee." After a few minutes, I returned with two steaming mugs and handed one to Wanda Sue.

"Don't worry none. Your love for Cole will make them little life adjustments a breeze." She raised her mug in a silent toast and then took a deep swig. "Trust me, it'll happen like that."

A breeze? Sounds more like a tropical storm. Or even a hurricane. I gulped my coffee, causing it to burn my mouth on the way down. Sputtering, I tried to inhale a few cooling breaths.

"You okay, girl?"

Still coughing, I nodded. "Enough about me. How are you doing after all the trauma today?"

"Surviving, I guess." She gave a visible shudder. "I've never seen anything like that before . . . poor Bucky. After Madame Geri took me home, I took myself a little rest and checked my blood pressure with one of those cuff thingies. The apostolic pressure was just a little high."

Did she mean the BP Holy Scale? Nah. "You might want to check in tomorrow at the island walk-in clinic and have the nurse-practitioner look you over."

"Will do, especially 'cause I think my stress levels may stay pretty high with life changes looming. Whatever happens to me, I've got to keep my Dixie-chick cool and be prepared."

Huh?

She set down her mug and held up the orange coveralls. "I got these from my friend, Betty Lou, who did time for grand theft auto."

"She stole a car?"

"Not really. She bought it from her nephew. She thought he just gave her a good deal. Turns out he'd carjacked some guy in another state and then sold it illegally to Betty Lou. When the police picked her up, they didn't believe her story."

I was downing my coffee rapidly, hoping the caffeine jolt would help me make sense of Wanda Sue's story. "And?"

"Well, she did three months in prison before the nephew turned up and told the truth. Then she got out. She got the island attorney to sue, got a lot of money, and bought a fancy condo in Lauderdale." My landlady paused and sighed. "But this hideous outfit is what she had to wear when she was in the slammer." She threw down the rumpled, orange, cotton coveralls, and a button popped off.

I wrinkled my nose. The pants smelled like an armpit. Pukey-colored and baggy, even Kate Moss would look like Ugly Betty in that getup.

"You see what I mean? This is what I'll be condemned to wearing if I go to jail for Bucky's m-murder." She choked back a sob. "I can't be seen dead in these things; my little grandson, Kevin, will be haunted by the image of his granny-convict."

I guess orange is the new black.

"We've already established that you're not going to prison," I said in a firm tone. Personally, I thought the other aspects of being in jail, such as living behind bars or eating crummy food or sharing a cell with *a real criminal* would outweigh the coveralls, but we all have our priorities. "I won't let that happen to you. *Promise.*" I reached over and squeezed her hand briefly (and kicked the coveralls back in her direction).

"I'm counting on it." She offered me a tremulous smile.

I leaned back in my chair, coffee mug in hand. "I have to ask this, Wanda Sue. You didn't see or . . . do anything, when you went back to the town hall?"

Her eyes kindled with indignation. "How could you even think that? You've known me nearly three years, and have I ever given you reason to believe that I could do harm to another person?"

"No, no, of course not." I added hastily, "It's just that . . . well, Detective Billie said that you dated Bucky, and had sort of a bad breakup . . ." I hesitated.

"So?"

I glanced down at the swirling darkness in my mug. "He

might've said something like you threatened Bucky with a frying pan and he filed a complaint against you."

Wanda Sue retrieved the crumpled coveralls and folded them on her lap. But she didn't answer.

"So, it's true?"

"Not exactly." She picked at the rough material.

"Which part?"

"Maybe it's an itty-bitty true." She held her thumb and forefingers about two inches apart. "But I never intended to actually hit him. You know us southern women. We're passionate about our men, especially when they're cheatin' on us."

I set my cup on the coffee table. "I'm all ears."

She took in a deep breath and let it out slowly in one long, dramatic sigh. "All right, I'll give you the whole story: I was going through one of those life phases a few years ago, before you came to the island, and I felt middle age creeping up like a shadow at my heels. Then Bucky started showing interest in me at the town-hall meetings, and . . . well, he swept yours truly off her feet with 'wining and dining' and little gifts. It wasn't that serious—more like the time you were dating Pop Pop."

"I wasn't *dating* Pop Pop."

"Of course you weren't, honey." She gave me a knowing wink. "Anyway, things were going along pretty good, when I started seeing another side of Bucky."

"Mean temper?"

"Ladies' man." She pursed her mouth.

"Bucky with the Bad Comb-over?" The words came out before I could stop myself.

"Oh, Lordy, his baldness just seemed to make him more attractive to women—that and the cowboy boots. Women just couldn't resist him. And it wasn't like he was trying too hard to fight them off, if you know what I mean. I could barely stand it after a couple of months. Then, one day, I was frying up some ham and collard greens at his place when some floozy called him. Right then and there. Can you believe that? I threw the frying pan on the floor and stomped out."

"Why did he file a complaint?"

"Oh, the grease must've splashed on his shirt." She sighed. "After all of his lyin', I was glad to get him out of my life."

"I'll bet," I chimed in, but was still having trouble seeing Bucky as a Don Juan. "Now the frying-pan incident is explained, who do you think might've hated Bucky enough to kill him? I mean, did he steal other men's wives?"

"Not that I can recollect."

"Was he dating anyone new? Nick Billie said he was seeing a woman in Paradisio."

"That ended early this year from what I heard on the island grapevine." She gave a knowing nod. "There was also some scuttlebutt that he might've been seeing a new girl, but . . . I don't know. It's probably just more gossip."

Maybe Coop had a line on that one since he worked so closely with Bucky.

"When is the grapevine ever wrong, except about Pop Pop and me?" I queried. "Dish."

Wanda Sue leaned forward, cupped one hand around her mouth, and whispered, "Destiny Ransford."

"What? Miss Buttoned-up, butter-won't-melt-in-her-mouth banker? That's an unlikely duo, if I've ever heard of one."

"I told you; Bucky is . . . uh . . . was a chick magnet."

I digested this info for a few seconds. "Now that you mention it, I did notice that he was protective of her during that fish fight at the town-hall meeting."

"Maybe it's true then." She tucked the coveralls in her large bag.

Kong trotted up and nuzzled against my leg and I reached down to stroke his soft fur between his ears. "I'll head over to

Shoreline Bank tomorrow morning and question Destiny—"

Just then, a knock on my door interrupted our conversation. "Cole. It's our date night," I explained to Wanda Sue. Why didn't I sound more enthusiastic?

"Where's your engagement ring?"

"Um . . . I put it away for safekeeping." *More lies.* Setting Kong down, I fluffed my curls and swung open the door.

Uh-oh.

Cole stood there, and next to him was Nick Billie, and they were both dressed to the nines.

Dating double trouble.

Chapter Six

For a long, long moment I could only stare; my motor mouth was in neutral with the parking brake on. Two hunky men stood at my door, one of them my fiancé: Cole, looking like a surfer dude ready for a hottie at the beach competition with his long hair combed back, a dark Hawaiian shirt, and chinos. The other one: Nick Billie, looking just as sexy with the black hair, black suit, and the edgy elegance of Fitzgerald's Gatsby.

How many women have this kind of delicious dilemma? Certainly not a girl like me.

Breathless, I stammered, "What are you b-both doing here?" *Lame.*

"We had a dinner date at the Starfish Lodge, babe." Cole produced a bouquet of wildflowers with delicate daisies and sprigs of greenery.

"And I came by to show you my preliminary report on Bucky McGuire's cause of death," Nick held up a sheet of legal-sized paper.

Sad to say, the latter sparked my interest the most as I took the flowers from Cole. "The medical examiner worked pretty fast on that one," I commented.

One side of Nick's mouth quirked upwards. "With the right kind of . . . persuasion, you get results fast."

"Is this about that guy who keeled over in a tilapia tank?" Cole asked. "When did it happen?"

"Right after the town-council candidate debate earlier today."

I plucked a few petals from the blossoms, trying to restrain myself from snatching the report out of Nick's hands. "Oh, and Wanda Sue found the body."

"Lordy!" she moaned from inside. "I'll be in those orange coveralls by lunchtime tomorrow!"

Nick's brow knitted in a frown. "Orange coveralls?"

"It's a long story. Just take my word for it that she's been watching one too many prison shows on TV." Checking over my shoulder, I noticed that her face had a pale cast (in spite of the canary-yellow hair). Then I turned back to Cole. "I can't just leave here while she's still so upset. Would you mind—"

"Let's make it a foursome tonight for dinner," he proposed, smiling into my eyes. "There's no reason why we can't share our evening at the Starfish Lodge with Wanda Sue and Nick just because we're engaged. Share the joy. Then Wanda Sue won't be alone, and Nick can give you his information. Just don't talk death and autopsies the *whole* evening, okay?" He kissed my cheek, a sweet brush of his mouth.

"You're on, if Wanda Sue is up to it." I hugged him, but my glance met Nick's over his shoulder. Something flared in the depths of his obsidian eyes. *Jealousy?* I couldn't tell, but it thrilled and disturbed me at the same time.

I set the flowers inside my Airstream, and Wanda Sue appeared at my side, purse in hand.

"Why, you sweet ole thing, Cole. I didn't want to be all on my lonesome tonight, what with all the fuss over Bucky's . . . uh . . . deceasedness." Sniffling, she reached into her purse, and I thought she was going to produce a Kleenex. Instead, she pulled out another "Elect Wanda Sue for You!" button and pinned it to his shirt. Then she fastened one on my dress. "All that ruckus aside, I can't waste any campaign opportunities. People might see us at the restaurant."

"I assume you don't have another flare gun in that purse,"

Nick warned, but kept his tone light.

"Nope." Wanda Sue opened her bag wide and held it out for Nick to inspect. "Just the usual girl stuff: compact, mascara, lipstick, eye shadow, and blush, and a stun gun."

He groaned as she listed the last item. "You don't need a license to carry one of those, so I'm going to pretend that I didn't hear or see that."

Cole eyed her purse cautiously and gave it a wide berth as he helped me lock up my Airstream.

"I'll drive," Nick suggested, pulling his keys out of his pants pocket. "My truck should fit everyone comfortably."

"Sounds good." I'd been a passenger in Nick's sleek and sexy Ford F-150 only once, but I could still remember the soft leather seats and subtle hint of his aftershave lingering in the interior. Invoking my car psychoanalysis skills, I noted that Nick's truck said it was all-powerful and too hot to handle.

"I'll sit up front with our island cop, to ride shotgun," Wanda Sue pronounced as she hopped into the passenger seat.

No one responded.

"Hey, it was a joke," she protested. When Wanda Sue still didn't get a response, she sniffed and started fiddling with Nick's radio.

Cole opened the door behind the driver's seat and helped me in, as Nick eased himself behind the wheel. I peeped around the headrest to see if he had set Bucky's "cause of death" sheet on the console. *Damn.* He must have folded it in his pocket. Now I'd have to wait until we reached the restaurant before I could get my hands on it.

Cole seated himself next to me and slipped an arm around my shoulders.

"Hah. I found the Jammin' Country station." Wanda Sue snapped her fingers, then began tapping time on her thighs to some male singer with a baritone whiskey twang. "That Josh

Turner has got himself some pipes, and he knows how to use 'em." She sang along with some lyrics about a black train, but I didn't know the song. I preferred my music on the indie rock end of the spectrum.

Nick switched on the interior light and held up the paper. "Is this what you want?" Our eyes locked in the rearview mirror.

I nodded and grabbed the sheet before he could change his mind. "How did you get it so fast?"

"The medical examiner was going on a vacation cruise and wanted to clear up any open cases." Nick started up the engine and checked over his shoulder before he backed out of my RV site. He flashed a quick smile in my direction.

I couldn't help my matching response.

As I rested in the crook of Cole's arm, I could hear his heartbeat as I scanned Bucky McGuire's probable cause of death.

Okay, it should've felt weird to be snuggling with my fiancé while I read an ME's report, but, for some reason, it didn't.

Nick drove the short distance from the Twin Palms RV Resort to the Starfish Lodge on Coral Island Sound, but I hardly noticed. I was engrossed in the description of the size and shape of the wound that Bucky had received to the back of his head. It seemed like a blunt object had struck him a few inches below the left ear and left a six-inch gash.

Whoa.

I tried to think of every object in the town-hall building that could've created that type of wound.

"A big rock?" I pondered aloud.

"Huh?" Cole responded.

Nick glanced in the rearview mirror again. "No, a rock probably would've sliced the skin with a jagged line."

"You sure?"

"Yep." Nick pulled into the restaurant's parking lot. "The

weapon had to have a clean edge."

"Oh, for goodness sake, isn't it enough that I had to find his body?" Wanda Sue threw her hands up in exasperation. "I need a few hours to forget about that horrible scene. I'm already flashing back with PSST." She climbed out of Nick's truck, and we all followed suit.

"She meant PTSD," I whispered to Cole as we made for the restaurant's entrance. I shoved the paper in my hobo bag, but my thoughts still swirled around what I had just read. "I won't bring it up again for the rest of the night. I promise."

"Good. Stone crab-claw season just started, and I want to enjoy my meal," Wanda Sue said as we entered the Starfish Lodge. A long, low building, the lodge was originally part of a turn-of-the-century utopian commune complex that had gone bust. It boasted heart of pine floors and a coral rock fireplace, but no communers, just diners.

My vow of silence on Bucky's cause of death lasted through our nachos appetizer platter and seafood entrées. But, by the time my Key lime pie dessert arrived, I couldn't contain myself any longer, and I mentioned possible suspects in Bucky's murder (which it appeared to be now).

At that point, Wanda Sue perked up over the sight of her cheesecake. "I guess there's no avoiding the subject of Bucky's death but, if you ask me, I think Destiny Ransford is a prime suspect. I'd arrest her for those boring suits she wears. There oughta be a law against a woman who dresses dowdy."

"Unfortunately, there's no Dull Dress Law," Nick commented over his coffee—no dessert for him, thank you very much, which was probably how he maintained the trim and muscular physique. I was digging into a large piece of my pie with its graham-cracker crust and whipped-cream topping.

"Destiny and Bucky were arguing right before the town-hall meeting, and it wasn't over 'bike path clean-ups,' if you get my drift," Wanda Sue admitted after downing a forkful of her cheesecake.

I paused, my fork halfway to my mouth. "What? You didn't tell me that."

Nick sipped his coffee. "Or me."

"Sorry. It slipped my mind till now, on account of the prospect of going to jail and having to wear orange coveralls." She gave a helpless shrug. "Anyways, I saw them behind the building near the big mango tree. I couldn't hear what they were saying, but their voices were raised and she looked ready to slap him silly."

"Lovers' quarrel?" I aimed a pointed look at Nick. "That might be a motive for murder."

"Let's back up," Nick began. "We're still talking probable cause of death."

"Bucky couldn't bash himself on the skull," I cut in.

"Hey, babe, I'm still eating." Cole pointed at his fresh fruit and low-fat yogurt bowl. He looked down at his forkful of healthy, low-calorie dessert and grimaced. "Kinda lost my appetite."

"Was it the 'bashed-in skull' comment?" I asked.

"Yep." He pushed the plate away.

I reached over and squeezed his hand. "I guess I'm still big-time dazed over Bucky's death. And a little time obsessed about making deadline on this story since Anita eloped with Mr. Benton and left me in charge of the newsroom."

"Anita and Benton? Married?" Nick blinked a couple of times.

"Hard to believe, but true." I finished the last crumb of my pie.

"Don't worry, babe." Cole covered my hand with his. "It'll all work out. You just need to keep your Zen balance and meditate. Maintain your center and limit all this talk about death and murder. That kind of stuff creates a weird energy."

A little twinge of annoyance tugged at me. "I *like* talking about death and murder. It's part of my life at the newspaper."

"Um . . . sure." Cole cleared his throat and sat back.

"Mallie, you're like the Sally Fields character in that old movie, 'Absence of Mullet.' She tracks down a killer who's done in a sleazy union bigwig." Wanda Sue's voice was lit with admiration.

"I think it's 'Absence of Malice,' " Nick corrected.

"Don't I wish?" I set down my fork. "I say more mullet and malice all around if I could be a younger version of Sally Fields."

Everyone laughed and the awkward moment passed, but Cole kept his gaze on me while we paid the bill. I mentally kicked myself as we headed out of the restaurant and made the short drive back to the Twin Palms RV Resort. I shouldn't have been so short with him. Murder and mayhem weren't exactly his thing.

Once we were back at the Airstream, Wanda Sue retrieved her dreaded orange convict coveralls and left, leaving me standing outside in the cold with Nick and Cole. After a few minutes of mindless small talk, I returned Nick's report and he drove off.

Cole stood next to me as we watched Nick's truck disappear into the darkness like a wisp of smoke.

"He loves you," Cole said, his words quiet and still.

"Oh, no."

"Please." He grasped my ringless hand, feeling the empty spot where the engagement ring should have been placed. "The question is, do you love him? I know I let you down when I left you in Orlando, but I thought we'd moved past that when we got engaged. But maybe not. It's your call. But your not wearing the ring is a sign, isn't it?" He dropped my hand.

"I . . . uh, just don't have it on tonight," I stammered. So I didn't lie—just didn't tell the whole truth.

The silence stretched between us like an elastic band.

Cole turned away and then continued with his back to me. "Let's be honest, because we've known each other too long to lie. If you have feelings for Nick, you shouldn't marry me. That's the road to heartbreak." His voice broke on the last word, and he moved off in the direction of his van.

I felt like a total, complete heel.

Did I love Nick? Did I love Cole? Did I love them both?

A gust of wind whipped up the sand, stinging against my bare legs, and I retreated inside my Airstream. I locked the door and leaned against it with my eyes closed tightly, hoping to block out the mess I'd made of my love life. Tears stung against my eyelids, but I refused to give into the desire to have a good old-fashioned sob fest.

Something nuzzled against my ankle, causing me to open my eyes and look down at my teacup poodle gazing up at me with a puzzled expression in his eyes.

Scooping him up, I hugged him tightly to my chest.

"What do you think, Kong? Should I bite the bullet and jump into matrimony? Sandy and Anita seem happy." Scratching the back of his head, I moved into the bedroom area of my Airstream. "No answer, huh?"

I set him on the bed, shrugged out of my clothes and into my pajamas. Flipping on the TV, I found some mind-numbing old reruns of "Friends" as I nodded off to sleep with my pooch curled up next to me.

Tomorrow was another day, and maybe I'd find the answers I was looking for in the clear light of sunup.

The next morning, I awoke to the usual lavish attention of my pooch as he gave my face a few licks. Reluctantly, I peeped open one eye to check the clock and flopped back down when I saw the ridiculously early hour. "It's barely dawn. Go back to sleep."

Kong trotted over to the door and began scratching it with his paws.

So much for sleeping in after my hair-raising experiences yesterday.

I threw back the covers, felt the chill in my Airstream, and covered up again with my tattered quilt. Kong barked—short and piercing—his I-want-my-food-now signal.

Still I didn't move.

It was too cold, and I wasn't ready to face a new day yet.

Kong amped up his bark to a howl.

"All right." Wrapping up in my covers, I stumbled over to the thermostat, jiggled it a few times, and waited for the blast of heat to flood through my Airstream.

It didn't take long.

I threw on my sweats, an old wool scarf, and running shoes (time to store temporarily the Birkenstocks). I guess Wanda Sue's warning about my blood thinning after a year or two in Florida was true. Once the temperature dropped below seventy degrees, I started fantasizing about ski jackets and fur boots.

Bracing myself, I dashed outside and faced the biting wind coming off the Gulf while Kong happily sauntered around the sea oats, taking his time, as always, to find just the right spot.

Looking off to the east, I noted the sky had a bleary, gray cast, with darkish clouds and no visible sun rising. A dawn with no light.

That didn't bode well.

Shivering, I hurried Kong along and took refuge in my Airstream once again. From the warmth of my snug trailer, I completed my morning ritual: Kong's breakfast, a big pot of coffee and a bowl of Cheerios for me, followed by a hot shower.

After a brief curl fluff, I donned the Florida Roller-Coaster

Weather uniform of jeans, t-shirt, and sweater, so I could peel back the layers if the sun came out later. My morning routine for this time of year kept things simple (and cheap), but ready for the twenty-degree temperature spikes.

After my second cup of coffee, I headed out to my truck and completed the second part of my morning ritual: a quick stop at the Circle K for a fresh Krispy Kreme donut. After that, I was ready to face the world—and my job as Senior Reporter and Temporary Editor.

As I pulled into the parking lot of the newspaper, it occurred to me that, as per Wanda Sue's warning, my ritual would have to change if I married Cole. I'd have to share my pot of coffee, have a healthy breakfast of granola and fresh fruit, and skip the Krispy Kreme fix.

A little tug of panic rose up inside of me.

Cole and I had worked different shifts when we lived together in Orlando years ago, but now we'd share the mornings.

Every morning.

The panic increased to cold-sweat level, in spite of Rusty's frigid interior.

Time to get to work. I had a newspaper edition to get out in only two days and didn't have time for all of this second-guessing about my love life.

I opened my door, faced another blast of cold air, and ran for the building. Once inside, instead of the deserted, lonesome office that had greeted me yesterday, I was treated to the smell of a lovely pot of coffee (good), a pleasantly heated environment (better), and the sound of computer keys clicking—by Joe Earl (best).

My eyes widened in amazement. Had I wandered into bizzaro newspaper world?

He looked up from Sandy's desk. "I had to take a hammer to that thermostat to get it to work, and it still took almost an hour to warm up this place." Turning his attention back to the computer, he added, "I made coffee and picked you up a snack."

"Um . . . are you working here now?" I asked casually as I strolled over to the coffee pot and found a package of Island Blend java and a Krispy Kreme donut positioned on top of a napkin in all of its high-sugar glazed glory. *Nirvana.* My head swiveled back to Joe Earl in dazed disbelief. Was he for real?

"How did you know about my sugar addiction?" I leveled a severe glance in his direction. "And don't tell me it was the Abe Lincoln violin."

"Madame Geri told me."

Whew. I was worried that the violin had done a Ouija board rat-out on me.

"But I did come in to sketch out some historical details for Madame Geri's story about my violin. She's got a morning Tai Chi class." He started clicking the keyboard with rapid-fire, staccato taps. "I thought you might want a boost after the Bucky thing yesterday. The dude's comb-over was bad business, but he didn't deserve to die like that."

"True." I poured a cup of the Island Blend's finest and savored its strong, deep aroma. Then, when I took a deep swig, a grin spread over my face. Dark-roasted and full-bodied. Oh, baby. Joe Earl and I were office soul mates.

"You are on the payroll as of today," I said, gliding over to my desk as I took a bite out of my Krispy Kreme. The glaze just melted in my mouth, leaving a lovely aftertaste of cakey sweetness.

More Nirvana.

Joe Earl hit the print button. "I'm actually getting bored with my eBay business, so I thought I'd give this journalism thing a try and help out."

"That's how I got started; I guess we have something else in common: we don't believe in career planning." I flipped on my own computer as I finished off the donut.

"What's the point of trying to plan? You end up where you're supposed to be anyway."

"So true." I checked my e-mail and found ten messages from Liz Ellis. I hit the delete button without even opening them. The rest of my mailbox content comprised unsolicited bulk e-mail, unsolicited commercial spam, and a couple of cute notes from Sandy (also unsolicited) with honeymoon pictures of her and Jimmy in St. Augustine. I flipped through the photos of their radiant faces and I couldn't help but smile.

"It's all karma," Joe Earl added.

"You've been around Madame Geri too long," I said with a roll of my eyes.

"She knows her stuff." He leaned back in Sandy's chair and folded his arms behind his head.

"Watch those loose wheels."

"I fixed all the rolling chairs this morning. The screws just needed tightening."

My mouth dropped open. Then I scooted around in my chair and tilted it back and forth. It creaked, but didn't tip over. This was beyond Nirvana; I'd died and gone to office heaven with fresh coffee, a Krispy Kreme donut, and working furniture. What a change twenty-four hours can make.

Doldrums to delight.

Feeling buoyant, I thought maybe my wave of good luck would keep on rolling, so I whipped open my desk drawer, thinking maybe the diamond engagement ring might materialize, too.

The joy bulb dimmed. Still missing.

I shut the drawer with a sigh.

"Madame Geri has me researching everyone who's ever owned the Abe Lincoln violin. Just think, all of the people who touched the wood on the violin touched the soul of a dead president. Awesome."

"You bet." I checked the desk drawer just one more time. *Nada.* "Just curious . . . um . . . while you were doing your Mr. Fixit thing around here, did you happen to find . . . a piece of jewelry?"

"Did you lose something?"

"Maybe."

"No jewelry. But I did find a few Snickers bar wrappers and empty Reese's cups under the chair cushions."

"They're probably leftovers from when Sandy was on her all-chocolate diet. She gained five pounds." I brushed a stray donut crumb off my jeans. "That was it?"

" 'Fraid so, but I've got a metal detector at home," he suggested. "I can go get it after lunch and hunt around the office."

"Oh, don't bother. It'll turn up." I hoped so, but doubts stirred inside—along with the thought that losing it was a sign. "Keep working on Madame Geri's story, but I think Bucky McGuire's death is our lead, especially if it turns out to be foul play. And I definitely want to interview Destiny Ransford today. Her name keeps coming up."

"I already pulled some info from his website, 'Bucky's Landscaping: I Take Care of Weeds and Dirty Deeds'." He reached over and handed me a hard copy of the home page. The company logo appeared to be a green-faced lizard man pushing an old-fashioned lawnmower.

"Catchy." The up-front close and personal pictures of Bucky were even worse: full-length shots of him wearing a dirt-encrusted t-shirt and jeans, holding up some kind of weed-whacker. "I thought the so-so economy had driven down landscaping prices. But look at this. Bucky charged five hundred bucks a month during season to cut the grass."

Joe Earl shrugged. "He's one of the few guys on the island who'd do that work, and . . . it seems that the female clients liked him. Their testimonials on the site were majorly good."

"Apparently, his employees felt the same. When I stopped at his house last night, I ran into one of his workers, Coop Naylor. He was trimming some bushes around Bucky's house and seemed pretty torn up about his death." I scanned the website pages, noting phrases like "Bucky McGuire is a wonderful landscaper," "There truly is no job too dirty," and "Hire him today" from clients.

"Is this Coop?" Joe Earl swung the computer screen in my direction and pointed at the lizard man image in the logo. "It looks like the lizard scales spell out 'Cooper' along the tail."

I squinted, then nodded. Sure enough, it was the same guy I met last night, except, of course, that he wore a lizard costume and had painted his face green. "And I thought I had it hard when Bernice forced me to wear stupid t-shirts. At least I never had to dress up like a reptile for a logo."

"I kind of like it." Joe Earl tilted his head left and then right, looking at Coop the Lizard Man from different angles. "He looks cool."

"Did you find any negative comments about Bucky on the website? They might give us a lead on someone who had a bone to pick with him." Flipping through my hard-copy pages, I found another gem of a Bucky photo, this time with no shirt at all and holding up a pair of long-bladed hedge clippers in one hand and a clump of weeds in the other.

"Just a few tirades by some woman named Liz Ellis. She wasn't happy with Bucky's landscaping services around her house, and she says so in pretty negative terms."

"Ohmigod, I know her. She came by the *Observer* office yesterday claiming that someone was killing the plants at her nursery. I just brushed her off, thinking she was a garden-variety nutso—no pun intended—and she's been e-mailing me obsessively ever since." Flipping back to the home page printout, I found several entries posted by Liz in the "testimonials" sidebar. No glowing comments here, to say the least. I spied the terms "rip-off," "cretin," and "want my money returned—or else." The last entry even included some creative obscenities. "She does a lot of name calling here about Bucky not taking care of her yard, but she doesn't mention if he was tending to her nursery as well."

"Is she credible?"

I flipped open my cell phone and slid it across Sandy's desk. "Scroll down to the e-mails that she sent me in the last twenty-four hours and you tell me."

He scanned through the messages with lightning speed, then handed the phone back to me without a word.

"She might be nutty as a fruitcake, but I still might interview her. You never know. Crazy people notice things, and I might be able to smooth things over with her lawsuit threat."

He aimed a skeptical glance in my direction. "I'd better have an attorney lined up."

"Anita already has one for the *Observer.* Believe it or not, people come out of the woodwork to sue newspapers, even a little island weekly." I moved Liz's e-mails to the "save" file, just in case she did follow through with her pledge to take legal action. "Anyway, this morning is my date with Destiny . . . Ransford, that is." My attempt at humor fell flat since Joe Earl didn't respond at all. "She was dating Bucky and was seen quarreling with him right before the town-hall meeting."

"Maybe he was leaving her for one of his landscaping groupies," Joe Earl supplied.

I raised my brows. "You think?"

"Maybe."

"Now that you're working here, see if you can put together a list of Bucky's clients from the ones who gave their names on the website. It might be there was someone else in his life besides Destiny."

He turned back to Sandy's computer screen and started clicking on the keys.

"No, wait, do a quick search on Destiny first, just to see if there's anything I should know before I talk with her. You'd be surprised who has a rap sheet."

"Not really."

For the umpteenth time this morning, I thanked my lucky stars (and the Abe Lincoln violin—I admit it) that Joe Earl had appeared at the office in my time of dire need. With his help, I just might be able to pull off this Editor/Senior Reporter gig and put together a kick-ass headline.

Someone banged loudly on the front door, and I jumped. "Oh, jeez, it's Bernice." I motioned her in, but she thumped her fist on the door again, repeatedly.

"All right, already!" I yelled out as I strode over to the door. Swinging it open, I clenched my teeth as a cold blast of air hit me. "Why you can't open the door yourself—" I broke off as I saw the reason why. She cruised past me still wearing the leather pants, with the addition of a "Girls Gone Wild" sweatshirt, and pedaling an "adult tricycle," the kind retirees rode around the island.

Her handlebar caught on the door jamb, and she ripped out a piece of wood but kept going, her wig flying full sail.

"Nice three-wheeler." Joe Earl glanced over briefly. "My granddad has one of those."

"Sounds like he's part of the 'geezer cool' set, just like me." Bernice took a few turns around the office, scratching the side of my desk and making tire marks on the carpet. "The bicycle bandit tried to steal this little gem from the Sunset-by-the-Sea Retirement Village just down the road. But he didn't make it past the shuffleboard courts before the oldies hopped on their scooters and started to chase him down. One of my sources who lives there texted me, and I arrived just in time to see the bandit ditch the bike and flee on foot. In all the commotion, I helped myself to the cycle and rode it here."

"You should've called Nick Billie. That bike is evidence," I pointed out.

She whirled around my desk, sideswiping the file cabinet. "I already did, and said I was bringing the evidence to him."

I groaned and scooped up the trash cans before Bernice and her Mean Geriatric Machine took them out. "If you break something in this office, you own it, and you have to fix it."

"I'll take my chances. It's too cold to give it a test drive outside." She headed toward Anita's cubicle and squeezed the brakes; they made a screeching sound, but they didn't slow her down.

"Bernice! Stop!" I shouted, clutching the remaining trash can to my chest.

"I can't! There's something wrong with the hand brakes." She pumped them for all they were worth, but she still kept rolling forward at the same speed. The tricycle's wide front tire rammed into the glass wall and shattered it, the force of the impact causing one of the back wheels to fall off.

Bernice was going down again.

Chapter Seven

I shouted something like "Thar she blows" as one side of the three-wheeler broke down. Bernice teetered precariously for a few moments, then tipped over into the pool of broken glass. Luckily, most of the window held—except the section where the wheel hit.

"Don't move, Bernice." I dropped the trash can and rushed over to her. "If you thrash around, you might get cut up from the glass."

Joe Earl picked up the phone. "I'll call the repair guy—his number is taped to Sandy's desk."

"Hold it . . . we may need 9-1-1 first." I checked her pulse, not sure about the medical procedure for an adult tricycle accident. "Are you okay?"

No response.

"Bernice?" I found a heartbeat. "Can you open your eyes?"

"Of course I can, you dummy." She raised her eyelids and brushed off a few pieces of glass that littered her faux-fur jacket. "I've had worse wrecks than this one."

"She's fine." I helped Bernice to her feet, checking her over for any cuts. "No scratches. No blood."

"I think I bruised my hip." Bernice massaged her right side and winced.

"You're lucky if that's all that happened," I spat out, then turned to Joe Earl. "Nix the 9-1-1 call."

He grabbed the Post-it note and punched in the repair guy's number.

"That was some kind of rush, slamming through Anita's office window like that." She eyed the spider web-like crack in the glass wall and chuckled. "Anita is going to be royally pissed off. Hey, I might slap the wheel back in place and take another run at it."

I held both arms out as a protective shield in front of Anita's office. "No! You've done enough damage for one morning. Besides, you're going to need to explain your story to Nick, and then start writing it for the *Observer.* We've got only two days to make deadline, and an eyewitness account of a bicycle-hijacking trumps the Abe Lincoln violin story."

Bernice righted her blond wig with a gleam in her eye. "You mean I might scoop that phony psychic and bump her from the front page?"

"You bet," I lied. "Why don't you take my desk and start working on it? I'm heading out to interview Destiny about the Bucky McGuire story."

Shrugging, Bernice strolled over to my desk, giving the tricycle tire a kick en route. "Stupid bike."

"Bernice, did you just destroy a crucial piece of evidence?" Nick Billie stood in the doorway, arms folded across his chest as he beheld our little corner of chaos: the broken-down tricycle, smashed-up glass window, and guilty look on my face.

"I swear I was riding the bike to the police station," Bernice protested. "It sort of steered itself into the office."

Nick didn't move. "You realize it's against the law to tamper with the scene of a crime."

"It wasn't my fault. The bicycle bandit was trying to get away with the trike; I helped to stop him, along with the retirement-home seniors. When he jumped off the cycle, the oldies followed him, and I confiscated the three-wheeler." Bernice thumped her chest in pride.

I held my breath, mentally calculating whether our liability policy covered Bernice's actions.

"I swear it's true." Bernice gave a Girl-Scout salute.

"All right. You're off the hook this time, but only because the Sunset-by-the-Sea folks corroborated your story," Nick finally said, motioning one of his deputies into the office. "Brad, wheel it over to the station."

Grim-faced, Deputy Brad hoisted up the trike and pushed it out of the office.

"Hey, Nick." Joe Earl waved his iPhone.

"Did they catch the bandit?" Bernice inquired, leaning on my desk.

"No, but the Sunset seniors gave a detailed description of him." Nick remained in the doorway. "We've got a pretty good idea who did it."

Bernice's face brightened. "Could I get an interview with you? I'm writing a story on the bandit—"

"No." He swung his glance in my direction. "I assume Anita and Benton are still out of town?"

"Yep. They're still honeymooning in downtown Detroit," I admitted with an arm sweep of the office. "Joe Earl and Bernice are my . . . temps till she returns—along with Madame Geri."

Nick muttered something unintelligible and left.

Whew. Another lawsuit dodged. "I'm heading over to Shoreline Bank to talk to Destiny." Grabbing my hobo bag, I started to leave the office.

"The repairman will be here in half an hour to fix the window." Joe Earl slipped his iPhone into the belt holster. "I'll tag along with you, Mallie."

"That's not such a good idea—" I began.

"No way am I hanging around the office with this crazy woman. Besides, I dug up some info on Destiny that I can tell you on the way."

I pushed open the door. "After you."

He grinned.

"I object to being called 'crazy' by a kooky computer nerd who thinks a violin sends him messages from Abe Lincoln," Bernice commented as she settled in at my desk. "You're on shaky ground yourself, kid, especially since the violin hasn't told us much of anything."

Joe Earl mumbled something that sounded like "old bag" as he preceded me out. She shouted back, "Geek freak," before I let the door slam shut.

As we emerged from the office, I was pleasantly surprised to note the wind had died down, and the gray clouds had dissipated. I turned my face up to the sun for a few moments, feeling a tiny ray of warmth.

"What's the story with Bernice?" Joe Earl asked.

"Tainted gene pool. When she was the temporary editor of the *Observer,* she made us share the office with a tree stump to get new advertisers."

"Huh?"

"Never mind. Just be happy that you haven't had to deal with her sister and my boss, Anita."

We trooped over to my truck and, happily, Rusty started up on the first crank, and we were on the road in no time. "So, what did you find out about Destiny?"

Joe Earl pulled out his iPhone again. "She's in her late twenties, was born in Tampa, went to the University of South Florida. Majored in business. After her graduation, she went to work for Shoreline Bank and moved to the Coral Island branch three years ago when she was promoted to assistant manager. The basics were pretty easy to find since she's on LinkedIn."

"Sounds pretty run of the mill." We passed Deputy Brad, still pushing the tricycle along the bike path. I honked and waved.

He didn't look up.

"It gets more interesting when you go to her Facebook page; it has a picture of her in a black leather cat suit, holding a whip and a pair of handcuffs." He flipped open the file and I caught a brief glance of Destiny the Catwoman. "She's got a slightly different name—Dusty Ransford—but I cross-referenced her background. It's her."

"Wow. Maybe that's the getup her bank makes her wear to drum up mortgage applicants. It'll sure get people's attention," I said, still dazed as I remembered her buttoned-up appearance at the town-council meeting. Was no one on this island what they appeared to be at first sight?

"The caption says 'Halloween, 2012,' but it looks to me like she might be one of those dominatrix chicks. Leather, whips, handcuffs—the whole nine yards of bondage. Maybe she's into all that junky-gunk."

"And maybe it was just a Halloween costume that she just never took off her Facebook page." I flexed my hands on the wheel and tried to focus on the road, attempting to expel the image of Miss Whiplash from my mind. "Anything else on Destiny besides the 'kinky boots' stuff?"

"Just that she had an aging mother who lived on the island; she died ten months ago."

"Sad." I frowned, promising myself that I'd call my mother this evening. "I have to give you credit for some speedy research. It usually takes me half a day and a couple of phone calls."

He shot me a "duh" glance. "Everything is out there if you know where to look—and have a smart phone."

"Guess so." I looked down at my "dumb phone" resting on my lap. Maybe it was time to upgrade and take a course on "Investigating with Your iPhone," especially if I wanted to keep the title of Senior Reporter. "Anything suspicious that might link her with Bucky's death?"

"Not so far."

"At the town-council meeting, Destiny seemed kind of straightlaced. You know, a manager type. I still can't quite see her with Bucky, and I certainly can't see her as some kind of thrill-seeking dominatrix chick." It didn't fit.

"I'm just reporting the facts." Joe Earl slipped his iPhone back in place.

I pulled into the Shoreline Bank parking lot, and cut off the engine.

"Thanks." I gave him a brief smile.

Joe Earl and I climbed out of my truck and headed for the building. A smallish, wooden structure, it had been painted pale green, the color of cash, with dollar signs stenciled on the stuccoed walls. A huge banner graced the entrance with palm trees and more dollar signs in the background, saying "Welcome New Customers!" *Big bucks decorating.* I had a mad moment of thinking I'd open a savings account, but then I realized that I had no money to put in one.

A woman came barreling out, head down, and ran smack-dab into me.

I stumbled back and realized it was . . . Liz Ellis.

"You!" She pointed her finger at me. Her bleached blond hair had been scraped up into a messy bun, and she wore an ankle-length, black tank dress with a flip-flop embroidered on the front. The wild expression in her eyes had been replaced with . . . sadness.

"Hi, Liz," I said with a halfhearted little wave.

"Are you following me? Snooping around?" she demanded. "Because, if you are, I'll just add it to my list of grievances that I'm going to give the island attorney when I sue you."

"Of course not." Cray Cray. "Joe Earl and I are here on newspaper business."

She gave him a contemptuous once-over. "Now you're

embroiling some kid in your half-baked journalism—"

"Hardly," I cut in before she could say something else that would really tick me off. "And just to show you there are no hard feelings, I rethought your story idea on the plant killer and would like do an interview—"

"Not today." A tear slid down her cheek. "I'm too broken up about Bucky."

"Bucky?" Joe Earl spoke up.

She shot him a venomous glance. "None of your business, kid."

My radar perked up instantly. Was it possible that Liz's angry entries on Bucky's website hadn't just been about her dissatisfaction with his landscaping services?

A woman scorned? Could she be?

I reached out a hand and touched her arm. "Liz, everyone on the island is shocked over Bucky's death, especially those people who knew him well."

She swiped at the tear with the back of her hand. "He was a good man—in spite of his flaws."

Nodding, I continued, "Are you talking about his landscaping? I know you weren't completely satisfied—"

"Hah! You *have* been snooping and prying into my life." She narrowed her eyes and knocked my hand away. "I'm adding 'invasion of privacy' to my potential lawsuit. My relationship with Bucky is *my* business."

"I wasn't suggesting—" I began.

"You'll be sorry that you tangled with me. I have rights." Liz stalked off.

As she drove off in her bright red Lincoln Town Car, Joe Earl let loose with a whistle of disbelief. "I guess that explains the e-mails."

"And then some." The Lincoln also screamed luxury, V8 power, and nineties-style status. I would've pegged her as a

Chevy Impala kind of woman, but my car psychoanalysis wasn't always foolproof.

"Looks like there might've been something between her and Bucky," Joe Earl commented.

"She's definitely going on our list. The trick is going to be getting her to talk without her slapping a restraining order on us."

The automatic glass doors slid open, and we strolled into the bank. The interior boasted a low-key, island atmosphere with mint-green paint, lots of wicker furniture, and potted plants. Even better, a coconutty smell permeated the room, light and pleasant, along with low-volume reggae music.

I was definitely going to open a savings account here, once I had a few bucks set aside.

Scanning the room, I noted two customers at the teller's window and an office to the left with a sign that read "Destiny Ransford—Assistant Manager and Mortgage Officer." Moving in that direction, I motioned for Joe Earl to follow. Destiny met us in the doorway, wearing a navy suit, pumps, and a phony smile, but her eyes were rimmed in red. She'd been crying—a lot.

Over Bucky?

Yet another woman distraught over the island Lothario's death?

"Hi, Destiny. I'm Mallie Monroe, Senior Reporter for the *Observer.*" I shook hands with her. "I don't know if you remember me or not, but I was covering the town-council meeting yesterday for the newspaper?"

She gave a shrug and murmured a "Nice to meet you," but I could tell she didn't know me from the proverbial man (or woman) on the moon.

"Oh, and this is my . . . uh . . . assistant, Joe Earl."

He waved his iPhone.

"If you could spare a few minutes, could I ask you some questions about yesterday?" I tried to keep my tone upbeat and chipper. "I'm writing a story on the upcoming election and town-council candidates."

Destiny hesitated for a few moments, then ushered us into her office and closed the door. She seated herself behind the mahogany desk, back ramrod straight, hair tucked firmly behind her ears.

Joe Earl and I slid into comfy, leather seats across from her that, unfortunately, made odd squishing sounds as we settled into the cushions. Trying not to squirm, I pulled out my Official Reporter's Notepad. "So, could you tell me why you decided to run for public office?" *Keep it light. Keep it simple.*

She cleared her throat. "I just wanted to give back to the island community, and show everyone that I care about local issues and local people . . ." Her voice trailed off, and I suppressed a yawn. Talk about a canned response. I could shelve that one behind the peas and carrots.

"What did you think of the debate?" I continued.

Her mouth tightened. "I'm not going to dignify what happened with any comment, except to say that I've never seen such an unprofessional display in my life—"

"From all of the candidates?" I cut in, scribbling in my notepad.

A shadow passed across her face. "Well . . . most of them."

I paused. "Even Bucky McGuire?"

She burst into tears.

Joe Earl and I exchanged glances.

"Ms. Ransford, I assume you know that Bucky was found dead at the town hall only hours after the council meeting," I said gently.

She gulped and nodded.

"Were you . . . close with Mr. McGuire?"

"Bucky and I were planning to get married at the end of the year." Tears rolled down her cheeks as she opened a desk drawer and retrieved a huge diamond engagement ring. The diamond was flanked by blue stones. "See this? A two-carat, marquis-cut diamond surrounded by sapphires. He gave it to me four months ago, but we decided to keep it private until after the election. Bucky McGuire was the love of my life."

"I'm very sorry for your loss." A pang of sympathy tugged at my heart—and a twinge of guilt that I hadn't protected my own ring as carefully.

"Me, too," Joe Earl added.

She dropped the diamond back in the drawer and locked it.

Smart woman.

"There is no reason why Bucky should be gone. He was in the best of health—his prime." Her tear-stained face fastened on me. "The island rumor mill has it that Bucky's death was suspicious. Is that true?"

"I can't say for sure." Okay, that part was true. "But, if you think there might've been foul play, do you know of anyone who might've wanted to . . . harm Bucky? Aside from his public argument with Travis Harper at the town-hall meeting, did you ever hear anyone threaten him?"

"Not really." Destiny's brows knitted in puzzlement. "Most everyone liked Bucky. He had a thriving business because he was so honest. That's one of the things I so admired about him." She sniffed and dabbed at her cheeks, then stopped. "Now that you mention it, though, there was a client of Bucky's who'd started harassing him about the landscaping around her house. She didn't like the types of bushes that he planted, or she wanted her grass cut an inch lower—that type of thing. The woman was completely bonkers and wrote some vicious comments on Bucky's blog."

"Liz Ellis?"

"Yes, that's her name!" Destiny's face kindled in anger. "She's some rich bitch with a big house in Paradisio who wanted more than her trees trimmed, if you get my meaning." The anger turned to an expression of disgust. "She's the only one I can think of, except for that horrible Wanda Sue, who's my opponent in the town-council race. Ugh. That piece of trailer trash was practically stalking Bucky after he broke up with her a couple of years ago. She seemed to calm down, until that flare-gun incident. Maybe she was even aiming for Bucky." Destiny crushed the handkerchief as her fingers curled into a fist. "She may have still been harboring hatred for Bucky because he rejected her."

"I've talked to her, but thanks for the input." I bristled inwardly at her comments, both about Wanda Sue and the merits of trailer life. My landlady was *not* a stalker, and not everyone who lives in a trailer is "trash." My sympathy for Destiny went down a notch. "I guess most people have secret aspects to their lives. Things that they normally hide from others, but maybe put on Facebook."

Her eyes cut to mine. "You're talking about that Halloween picture."

"It looks . . . provocative," I said.

"Sure does," Joe Earl chimed in.

A bright red flush spread across her cheeks. "Bucky liked the picture, but it was a Halloween costume, that's all, I swear. I wanted to take it off Facebook, but he didn't want me to. I guess that was a mistake." Anger fading, she began to sob quietly again.

"I'm sorry to have to ask these questions so quickly after losing your boyfriend."

Her shoulders shook as she rocked back and forth. "You don't know what that's like to have the person you care about most in the world just gone one day. The pain is almost too much to bear after losing my mother not long ago."

Joe Earl and I sat quietly, while Destiny cried. "Trailer trash" comment aside, it was heartbreaking to see someone in such a deep hole of grief.

"If only I'd been there with him, maybe I could've prevented his death," she said, slumping back into her chair.

"You have no way of knowing that," I said, shaking my head. "Until the police know exactly what happened, it's probably best not to speculate."

"I guess so." She covered the top part of her face with her hand and sighed deeply, sorrowfully.

I rose to my feet. "Maybe we should leave you to your grief right now." She was too distraught to give us any useful information at the moment, and I couldn't blame her. Her whole world had just been turned upside down, and she was still in a state of shock. "If you can think of anything else that you'd like to share with me, just give me a call." I placed my card on her desk. It was one of the new ones on which I had penciled in "Senior" above "Reporter."

Destiny grasped my hand before I could move away. "Bucky was a good man and, if it turns out that his death wasn't by natural causes, promise me that you'll help find who did him in." Her fingers tightened around my skin. "Justice needs to be served."

"I promise to do what I can." Sliding my fingers out of Destiny's grip, I gave her palm a little squeeze of reassurance before I let go. "Take care." I signaled for Joe Earl to exit with me. Once back in Rusty, I let out a shaky breath.

"That was intense," Joe Earl commented, setting his iPhone on the dashboard.

"And then some." I leaned back against the headrest, omming my "muggatoni mantra." Over-the-top emotion wasn't my thing, to say the least, especially when it involved the untimely death of someone. I flashed back to the scene at the town-hall meeting yesterday, conjuring up the memory of Bucky's good-ole-boy grin as he handed out the free fish.

Sad. Sad. Sad.

"Destiny sure seemed torn up." A shadow passed over Joe Earl's young face. "You think it was real?"

"She was hurting, that's for sure." Starting up the engine, I reflected on the look in Destiny's eyes as she glanced at the diamond; it was as if her world had suddenly lost all glimmer of hope. "But she may also know more than she let on. I mean, she was pretty quick to lay blame on Wanda Sue."

"Yeah."

We fell silent. Whatever Destiny's motivations, it seemed fitting to pay respect to that kind of loss. "Pitched past pitch of grief," as the poet Hopkins would say. I'd never really understood those words completely before, but I think I did now. Losing someone so suddenly created a gaping, black hole right in the middle of your life—a midnight of darkness and despair.

Silently, I turned left on Cypress Drive and noted the palm trees pass by in a blur of swaying fronds. The breeze had kicked up again, even though the temperature had turned almost balmy.

When I reached the island center, I checked my Mickey Mouse watch (a souvenir from my tenure there as a cast member—translation: theme-park drudge); it was nearly noon. "How about we hit that new island diner to throw off the funk?"

"You're on."

I headed south for another five minutes, and then spotted the retro Florida postcard-like sign, Cresswell's Retro Diner, and turned in. The parking lot was already crowded, but not crazy busy, which meant we could probably get a stool at the counter. The place had just opened, and it served my favorite meal of all time: a three-inch thick, old-fashioned, artery-clogging cheeseburger smothered in every condiment known to humankind.

Too bad I wasn't still on my restaurant critic gig. I would've given them five stars and glowing review for the thick-cut fries alone.

As I reached for the door handle, my cell phone rang.

Aunt Lily's name came up. "I have to take this, Joe Earl." As I flipped open my phone, I didn't even have time to tell my great-aunt "Hello" before she started in.

"Mallie, have you heard about Bucky?" she exclaimed. "I went to my quilting group this morning, and they told me that he keeled over in the tilapia tank at the town-hall building, and Wanda Sue found his body. I can barely believe it, even as I say it. Is that true?"

"Yes. I was going to call you this afternoon, but I just haven't had two minutes to myself." I filled her in on the events of the last twenty-four hours, hedging around any confidential details. "I'm working on a story about Bucky's death but right now, it's just initial interviews. I hate to ask this, but did you happen to pick up any tidbits from the quilters about him?"

"Not really." Her voice still sounded shaky. "A couple of them used his landscaping services and had no complaints. Some of them knew him socially from the Paradisio Food Pantry. I guess he donated pretty generously. And a couple of quilters who attended the council meeting yesterday raved about the tilapia giveaway. They said the fish fried up nice and crispy."

Damn. I knew I should've grabbed some for myself.

"I think he would've given Travis a run for his money for the council seat," she continued. "I heard a lot of the quilters say they were going to vote for him, in spite of the fracas at the meeting."

"I'm not surprised." Especially because he seemed to have a high female-appeal factor.

"It's all been quite a shock, and I'm just sorry that my last conversation with Bucky was so negative, but what could I do? He was beating his opponent with a fish carcass." A tinge of regret shaded her words.

"You were more than fair, Aunt Lily—and patient." I spied two more cars pulling into the parking lot. "Look, I've got to grab some lunch at the Cresswell's Diner, but I'll get back with you later—"

"Wait. I did hear one thing from one of Bucky's clients: I guess his landscaping rates had just gone up—almost doubled—even for established customers. She thought he might've been having financial trouble."

"That's interesting." Clutching my phone, I was torn between pressing my great-aunt for more information or getting in my order for those thick-cut fries. My stomach growled. My mouth watered. "Okay, I'll catch you later."

"I'm starving." Joe Earl hustled out of my truck, and I followed suit.

"Me, too." I could already taste the lip-smacking sea salt on the fries. "Make a mental note to investigate Bucky's financial statements. He might've been juggling some big debts."

"Gotcha," Joe Earl said as we headed in. "Looks packed."

"Don't worry. I know the owners." I inhaled one of my favorite aromas: the lovely smell of a sizzling grill.

With only ten booths and a half dozen stools at the counter, the diner was a small operation decorated with Florida deco posters and plastic alligators, harkening back to the boom days of the thirties, right down to boogie-woogie music in the background. Every table was filled, mostly with locals wearing "Coral Island Reeboks": fishermen's knee-high, white rubber boots. *De rigueur* for the well-dressed islander.

"Mallie!" a voice greeted me above the din of loud conversations. I smiled and waved. It was Nora Cresswell, wearing a brown and yellow print, vintage dress with her gleaming chestnut hair swept up in a French twist. Two years ago I had helped her escape from a dead-end job and saved her husband, Pete, from going to jail, and we'd been friends ever since. It was one of my success stories from the early Mixed-up Mallie days at the *Observer,* and I reveled in it.

Of course, from my present Senior Reporter status, that seemed ages ago.

I hugged Nora and then turned to introduce my companion.

"Oh, I've known Joe Earl forever. He set up our whole computer system for Pete at the marina." She gave him a hug, too, and then led us over to a couple of empty stools; the other four were occupied. She patted one orange, leather seat. "All I've got is the counter for now, but I can move you when a booth clears."

"I prefer it here." Grinning, I seated myself. As the song "Happy Days are Here Again," blared out through the restaurant, my smile upped a notch. "Any time I'm this close to the grill, I'm happy."

Nora laughed. "You got a ringside view for your burger and fries." She brushed back a few stray hairs from her forehead and handed Joe Earl a one-page, plastic-covered menu decorated with palm fronds and orange trees. "It's a limited selection, but Mallie always orders the same thing."

"You bet. And feel free to order anything up to five bucks for the *Observer* to reimburse you." I gave Joe Earl a wink, then checked out my fellow diners who were happily gobbling down their lunches. "Business looks good in spite of the 'tween season."

"We're bursting at the seams for breakfast and lunch. Couldn't be better," her voice sang out with the lilt of success as she pulled out an order pad and pencil from her pocket. "I might have to hire a third grill guy when season starts."

"Excellente."

"Joe Earl, what can I get you?" she asked, her pencil poised above the pad.

He studied the menu for a few moments. "I'll have a hot dog and Coke."

"Good choice. Our hot dogs are one hundred percent pure beef. No filler." She jotted down a few words. "One Mallie special and one bow-wow on a bun." Nora handed the slip to a young woman behind the counter; she was dressed similarly to Nora, but wore her hair in an angular, chin-length bob.

"How's baby Brian?" I asked.

"Well, since you asked . . . hardly a baby." Nora produced a picture from her shirt pocket. "He's two now. Pete has him at the marina with him in the morning, and I take him home in the afternoon when we shut down after lunch. Of course, I can't compete with fishing and boating with Daddy, but someone has to teach that boy to read more than a marine-parts catalog."

I looked down at the picture of Pete holding a small, sandy-haired boy in his arms, both of them beaming as they struggled to hold up a large, gray fish with black dots.

"That grouper is bigger than Brian." I laughed, handing it back to her.

Nora kissed the picture, then tucked it in her pocket and patted her shirt. "Every day with them is a beach day."

I nodded as we exchanged a knowing glance of how close she'd been to losing Pete. The near-tragedy made this life all that much sweeter.

"Oops. Just remembered that I left my phone in the truck. I'll be right back." Joe Earl sprinted out of the restaurant.

"Digital natives." I gave a helpless shrug.

"Is he working at the newspaper?"

"Sort of. Things are a little complicated right now, both

professionally and personally." I glanced down at my ringless finger, then at Nora again. Her brows lifted in surprise.

"Where's your ring, girlfriend?" Nora asked.

I mouthed the words, "Misplaced it," not wanting to say them aloud.

Her mouth dropped open slightly.

"I know. All kinds of stupid." I looked away from her. Love didn't feel like a beach to me, but more like a troubling wind stirring up the sand. And it wasn't just the misplaced diamond that made me feel guilty. Nora's love for Pete and her son shone out from every part of her being, and it was a total reproach of every second I didn't pony up to my true feelings. I felt her soft hand touch my arm. "Mallie, what's wrong?"

I swung my glance back. "Just the usual: love life stinks, newspaper in chaos, another suspicious death."

"Let's go with the last one—Bucky McGuire?"

Nodding, I patted the now-empty stool next to me. "You know Anita left for a . . . honeymoon" (still had a hard time getting the word out) "with Old Man Benton—"

"No!" Nora gasped and flagged down the girl behind the counter again. "Water over here, please." In seconds, a bottle of Pellegrino appeared.

"Only too true. It could be one of those bizarre facts in a *Guinness Book of World Records:* 'Crustiest Person in the World Marries Cheapest Person in the World.' Even worse, Anita just took off, leaving me in charge of the *Observer,* with only Bernice and Madame Geri to help out with the reporting. Thank goodness I've got a couple of stories with the bicycle bandit loose on the island, and Joe Earl's violin—"

"The one with the image of Abe Lincoln?" She crossed herself and took a long, deep gulp of water.

I groaned. "Not you, too?"

"I saw it on the Coral Island Facebook page, and it was freaky."

"That violin rocks." Joe Earl sidled up, iPhone in hand.

Ignoring him, I focused on Nora. "The violin and bicycle bandit are good filler stories, but my headline is going to be Bucky McGuire's death. What have you heard?"

"Everything from Bucky had a heart attack and fell on the town-hall tilapia tank, to Wanda Sue tried to kill him with a flare gun and knocked him into the tank, to my personal favorite: the tilapia jumped out of the tank and killed Bucky themselves." She joined her hands together and made a swimming shark motion while humming the music from *Jaws.*

"Hey, that might be my headline: Killer Fish Attack Islander," I said, trying to get a mental image of the tilapia in full-attack mode, but nothing came to me. "Just as an FYI, the flare-gun incident did happen, but it was during the town-council meeting. Wanda Sue swears the flare gun wasn't aimed at him, and I believe her, even though I was cringing on the floor at the time and couldn't really see what happened. She wasn't gunning for anyone, just trying to quiet things down."

"I bet that did the trick," Nora said with an amused expression.

"Pretty much."

The stool on the other side of me cleared, and Joe Earl took it. "She sounds like a kick-ass kind of woman."

"In platform shoes, no less," I added.

The guy working the grill placed a steaming cup of coffee in front of me. I inhaled the aroma for a few seconds, then took a sip and gave him a thumbs-up in appreciation. "Nora, you know everyone and everything on this island, so fill me in on Bucky. What's his story?"

She slipped her pencil behind her right ear. "What do you want to know?"

"First of all, from what I've heard, he seemed to be dating every woman on Coral Island. What gives with that?" I cradled my coffee cup between my hands. "I mean, let's be honest. He might've emoted a balding Billy Ray Cyrus appeal, but a chick magnet? I didn't see it, but I've observed two women reduced to tears today over him."

"Handyman Syndrome," Nora pronounced. "He could fix stuff around the house. Single women love that. I also heard he was a southern romantic, a flowers and chocolate kind of guy with a cowboy edge. Never underestimate the 'southern bad boy' swagger."

"With a *bad* comb-over," I muttered, still not getting the Bucky appeal. Shaking my head, I reached for my hobo bag. "Let me get my notepad—"

"I'm taking notes for you on my iPhone," Joe Earl cut in.

He was a gift from St. Bob of Woodward, the *Washington Post* patron saint of journalists.

"Okay. Let's just say for now I accept that Bucky was a country Casanova with a few disgruntled exes. Did he have any hit-you-on-the-back-of-the-head enemies?" I asked, distracted by the plates going by with juicy-looking, inch-thick burgers. *Yum.*

"Dunno. From what I've heard, most of the islanders liked him 'cause he had a reputation of doing an honest day's work."

"That's what his worker told me," I chimed in.

"Coop?"

I nodded. "What about Travis?"

Nora pursed her mouth. "Well, that's another issue altogether. I think they were friends in the past, but their relationship soured at some point after they started working together. All I know is they were business partners in the tilapia farm, then, something happened a couple of years ago—not sure what—and they dissolved the partnership. Bucky went out on his own to start a landscaping company, and he did pretty well from what I've heard."

"Yeah, we found only one negative review on Bucky's company blog," I said. Crazy Liz Ellis. And she hardly counted.

"Coop may know more about the falling out with Travis but, of course, the trick is to get him to remember it." She gave me a pointed glance, and continued. "I'd heard Bucky wanted to get out of the landscaping business and move on, but who knows? The island grapevine isn't always reliable." She stood up and smoothed down her dress. "He came in here for lunch a lot, and he always tipped the wait staff very nicely, so we were all upset to hear that he died like that in a fish tank."

"Sort of . . . creepy," I said with an inward shudder.

"Yeah."

Our conversation dwindled out at that point.

"Okay, enough of that talk. Let me check on your lunch." Nora gave me a quick pat and headed around the counter.

"Did you get all of that?" I turned to Joe Earl.

"Sure did."

"Let's hold off on questioning Liz Ellis and drive to Travis's tilapia farm after lunch. I want to talk with him first and get a feel for what happened to his partnership with Bucky. He seemed to be in a state of high pissed-offedness at the town-council meeting yesterday."

"Two-timer!" a voice exclaimed from behind me. "You're cheating on me and I won't take it anymore!"

Everyone in the diner turned and glared at me.

What did I do?

Chapter Eight

Quickly, I swiveled around to behold . . . Pop Pop Welch in his plaid dress shorts, golf shirt, and portable oxygen tank. A dapper sight. But his usually sunny expression had been replaced by a deep frown.

"Mallie, how could you do this?" He shook one bony finger at Joe Earl and me. "I thought we had something good going, and that you'd come back to *me* when the thing with that young whippersnapper, Cole, ended. But now you're dating a schoolboy!"

The lunchtime crowd began to murmur among themselves, and I shifted uneasily on my perch. This little scene would be all over Coral Island by this afternoon, and my reputation wouldn't fare well.

Mallie the Cheater strikes again.

"Pop Pop, are you taking your blood-pressure meds?" I asked in a calm voice, aware that most of the diners had probably already flipped out their cell phones and were texting as the events unfolded. And once the island grapevine was activated, the gossip spread with the speed of light.

"You were dating *him*?" Joe Earl's brows spiked at the same angle as his hair.

"Darn right, she was, sonny, and we had some great times together." His chin rose with pride as he adjusted the oxygen strap around the back of his head.

By sundown, I'll be framed as the island hussy.

"Pop Pop, this is Joe Earl. He's working temporarily at the *Observer.* That's all, and I'm still engaged to Cole." I patted the orange, leather seat that Nora had just vacated. "Why don't you sit down and join us?"

A slow smile of large, yellow teeth appeared. "Don't mind if I do." He hopped up on the stool, grabbed a menu, and positioned his oxygen tank under the counter. "I'll have the burger and fries, just like old times when we'd have dinner at Le Sink, isn't it?"

The other diners snapped their cell phones shut and went back to eating lunch. I could almost hear the collective sigh of disappointment thread through the room. *Hah.*

"We went there only once, and I was doing a food-critic review." I looked at Joe Earl and silently circled a finger around my ear, whispering, "Pop Pop has good days and bad days."

Pop Pop gave his order to the grill guy and then rapped himself on the forehead. "Tarnation! I forgot my wallet. I'm getting more and more forgetful every day."

"You can't order lunch if you don't have cash or credit," Grill Guy said.

"I'll buy his lunch. No problem," I hastened to add, not wanting to rile Pop Pop up again and provide the islanders more fodder for the gristmill about my love life.

"Thanks, Mallie." Pop Pop straightened his shirt collar and leaned toward me with a conspiratorial wink. "Pretty good 'jealous ex-boyfriend' act, huh? Old people have to be crafty to get a free lunch."

I glared at him.

"Miss, would you tell your 'date' that he can't do that with his false teeth." Grill Guy growled his disgust because Pop Pop had dropped his dentures in the nearest water glass—mine.

"Gross," Joe Earl exclaimed.

I pushed my glass in front of Pop Pop and said in as firm a

voice as I could muster, "You need to put the dentures back in place."

"Sure, toots. If I get a free dessert."

Grill Guy held up his burger flipper as if warding off the devil. "Done. And it's on me."

Pop Pop winked again as he fished around for his false teeth but, just when he'd retrieved them, they slipped through his arthritic fingers onto the floor. He swooped down to pick them up but elbowed his oxygen tank, which began to roll across the tiled floor. Watching in growing horror, I made a desperate grab for the tank and missed, but I managed to get a grip on the plastic hose.

"My tank!" Pop Pop exclaimed as he jumped off the stool. He tripped over the hose, and fell down.

"Call 9-1-1!" someone yelled.

"I'm speed dialing." Joe Earl was already making the call.

"That old guy went down, and his oxygen tank is *mine*!" An elderly lady tottered over and made a wild grab for it.

In one smooth motion, I yanked the hose and pulled back the tank. Unfortunately, she lost her balance and took a tumble, moaning that she'd broken a hip.

Pop Pop seized my ankle as he looked up. "Don't forget my burger. I can eat it in the ambulance."

Just like old times, all right.

Two hours later, the island paramedics had arrived, checked Pop Pop over, and pronounced him fine (the old lady unfortunately *had* broken a hip, and they took her away). Muttering curses under my breath, I loaded Pop Pop in the backseat of my truck. He chowed down on his burger (dentures in place again), clutching his oxygen tank with a possessive clasp.

"All I wanted was a lunch freebie," Pop Pop said, wiping off a trickle of ketchup from the side of his mouth.

"Just ask me next time." I headed back to the Twin Palms as fast as Rusty would go to drop off my "date." It was almost two o'clock and getting warm inside my truck now that the sun blazed down and my air-conditioning was on the fritz. I didn't want Pop Pop having heat stroke in my backseat.

"Speaking of food, I never got my hot dog," Joe Earl said. "My next meal should be free and charged to the *Observer.*"

"Deal." I glanced back at Pop Pop. "See what you started?"

No answer. He'd already nodded off and was snoring away.

A small reprieve. Focusing on the road, I chanted my "muggatoni mantra" again to re-balance my chakras. I'd apologized to Nora on our way out of the diner, but I figured it would be at least a week before I could show my face there again. After ten mantras, I was sufficiently centered and felt ready to tackle a conversation about the day's events thus far (minus the denture incident). "You know, Destiny Ransford never said what her future plans were with Bucky after they got married," I mused to Joe Earl.

"No, she didn't. If he was having money problems, maybe he wanted to close down the landscaping thing and start up a business with Destiny. She worked for a bank, so I guess she could get cheap loans."

"Maybe." I checked the mirror again to make sure Pop Pop was still dozing and not eavesdropping. His head was tilted back, mouth open, and eyes closed. All clear. "Another point: Destiny was the only one of three women—that we know of—who dated Bucky and held down a professional job."

"Not true to his type? That could be significant." Joe Earl rolled down his window, wiping his forehead. "It's heatin' up in here."

"Think cool thoughts. The AC is broken." I offered an apologetic smile. At any given time, I had a working heater or a working air conditioner, but not both at once. Hey, it was an old truck.

"I'll try." He stuck his head out the window. "And, if Bucky was having money problems, it might've been the reason he was dating Destiny and cut corners with Liz Ellis's landscaping."

I felt the sweat bead on the back of my neck, and I lowered my window, as well. "As Anita always says, 'Follow the money.' "

"What about this Travis dude?"

"From what I could tell at the town-council meeting, there was bad blood between them, way beyond just dissolving their business partnership. He got into a knock-down, drag-out fish fight with Bucky that was truly nasty." I turned into the Twin Palms. "And, just as a heads-up, Travis has quite a temper under that southern-gentleman veneer."

"I'll watch myself when we interview him."

Pop Pop stirred, opening his eyelids, and flapping his arms, sort of like a homing pigeon approaching the nest. "I must've dozed off. Sorry I missed the last part of our date, Mallie."

I glanced in the rearview mirror once more, ready to make a snappy retort, but I spied Pop Pop take a deep whiff of oxygen, so I refrained. Maybe he *had* stopped taking his blood-pressure medication and it was affecting his judgment (not stellar to begin with).

As I pulled up to the main office, Wanda Sue came jogging out in a matching tropical-print top and Capris with cork wedgie sandals. How she moved so fast in those three-inch platforms was beyond me.

The moment I parked, Pop Pop sprang out of the back seat and headed to his trailer, tank in tow. He waved good-bye.

"Hey, nice of y'all to tote him back here, but it's the least you can do after you jilted him again, Mallie." She propped one arm against my truck roof. "I heard tell that Pop Pop tried to re-stake his claim as your fallback guy at Cresswell's Diner, just in case Cole dropped out as the fiancé."

"Who told you that?" I thumped my steering wheel in frustration. "It just happened a few minutes ago."

"This is a small island, honey. I was getting texts from the time Pop Pop walked in. Is it true that he collapsed in a heap when he saw Joe Earl had already taken up the second-string role?"

"Those are bald-faced lies," I protested hotly. "First of all, Pop Pop didn't collapse. Some old lady tried to steal his oxygen tank, and he tripped over the hose while he was trying to hold onto it. Secondly, just to remind you, Joe Earl is now quasi-working at the *Observer.* He wasn't my date." I gestured toward him; he nodded. "Thirdly, we're investigating Bucky McGuire's murder, so *you* don't go to jail, remember?"

"Sorry. How could I forget?" She grimaced. "I've got that orange prison suit hanging in my closet as a reminder every day."

"I just wanted to set the record straight." Mollified, I cut off the truck's engine. "We're heading to Travis's tilapia farm to question him, but I wanted to ask if you remember why Bucky dissolved his partnership with Travis. Did that happen when you were seeing him?"

Wanda Sue tapped a little bongo beat on my truck, as if she were drumming up memories. "As I recall, they were tighter than two peas in a pod when I first starting dating Bucky, but then I started hearing them argue when I dropped by the fish farm—not raisin' their voices much—but still, kind of riled up. Travis had somehow taken over the whole tilapia operation, leaving Bucky with only his landscaping service. I never got more than snatches of conversations when I'd hear them fussing about feeding the tilapia, keeping up the fish tanks, customer orders, and stuff like that."

"Anything else?" Joe Earl inquired.

"Destiny Ransford." Her drumming stopped. "I heard her name mentioned a couple of times."

My eyes caught hers. "Wanda Sue, you told me last night that Bucky had been cheating on you. Do you think it was Liz Ellis or Destiny? Which one called your house the day of the frying-pan incident?"

"I can't say for sure 'cause maybe I've just blocked it out of my mind, but I think the phone call was from that Ellis woman in Paradisio," she admitted with a small shrug. "I'm long over that womanizing Don Johnny; he was nothing but trouble, God rest his soul."

"Thanks. One last thing. Could you make sure Pop Pop is taking all of his medications? He's acting a little weird, even for him." With a salute of gratitude, I started up Rusty again and steered back onto Cypress Drive. "Joe Earl, would you MapQuest Travis's tilapia farm?"

"Already did. Drive south past the island center, and make a right at Maria Drive; it's 1.3 miles down the road, near the mango farms."

"Try to be more precise next time." I pressed down the gas pedal, feeling the breeze lift my hair from the back of my neck. "You're better than having a GPS system, not that poor old Rusty could handle one of them." Needless to say, my aging truck had been built long before GPS was invented, and I couldn't see spending some of my meager salary on a portable unit. But what other vehicle could pull a 4,220-pound Airstream through the Smoky Mountains and emerge with its transmission intact?

"Where does Travis fit on the suspect list?" Joe Earl inquired.

"Pretty high, especially after I heard Wanda Sue's comments." My thumbs rubbed against the cracked plastic of the steering wheel. "Let's get some background on Travis's company. I think it's public, so we should be able to find a financial statement online through the Securities and Exchange Commission. That might give us a clue as to what happened to his partnership with Bucky, and why there was bad blood between them."

"Sounds like a plan." He checked the MapQuest again. "Then again, from everything I've read online about Travis, he seems more like a white-collar crime kind of dude. I mean, he might take over your company and even steal your girlfriend—but murder? I don't see it." He paused. "Maybe we should stop at the office and ask the Abe Lincoln violin again. It may have come up with something more concrete—"

"Than a bridal-magazine cover?" I finished for him. "Let's question Travis first; he might let something slip." There was no way in hell I was going to let a damned violin guide my investigation.

"You know, that violin is over two hundred years old, and it's been played by musicians all over the world. To think that some essence of them might cling to it isn't that farfetched. One of the owners supposedly played it at a concert in front of Lincoln, so who knows?" He turned and looked at me. "There are more things in heaven and earth than you've dreamed of, Horatio."

"Now you're playing unfair to use Shakespeare's *Hamlet* against me."

"High-school English, from what I remember."

"Okay, I'll give you that one, but I'm going to do my investigation the good old-fashioned journalist way: dig through the muck of information, harass people, and hope I get lucky." Considering my so-so luck during the last couple of murder investigations, maybe his suggestion wasn't completely bonkers. "The violin is our last resort."

I spied the sign for the Tropical Tilapia Farm and made a right turn, slowing down as Rusty lurched over a few potholes on the rough gravel and shell road. Joe Earl reached for a passenger-side strap, but it was long gone, so he braced himself against the dashboard.

"How does Travis haul fish on this road?" I said as Rusty thumped hard on a particularly deep hole.

"He probably has his own eighteen-wheelers for deliveries. The tilapia have to be moved in large, iced coolers from what I read."

"To keep them fresh?"

"Yep." Joe Earl inclined his spike-haired head. "They're grown in large tanks with a water-filtration system. It's really kind of cool. Anyone with a little ingenuity, some PVC pipe, and a plastic blow-up pool from Wal-Mart can start farming tilapia. It's a low-cost backyard business, if you start small." His voice upped a notch in enthusiasm. "The main problem is the filtration system. It has to be set up right or you've got a lot of dead fish. But if you keep the water fresh and put one male in a tank with a lot of females, you've got a lot of baby tilapia."

"And a potential moneymaker," I added, wondering if I could set up a little fish biz for fast cash behind my Airstream. Probably not, unless I could run it from a kiddie pool that was small enough to fit on my site. Not likely. As I turned onto a palm tree–lined entrance road, I spied several large, tent-like structures draped in canvas with humming generators on the side. My eyes widened. "I stand corrected: a big-time moneymaker."

I brought Rusty to a halt in front of the compound and sat there for a few minutes, taking in the breadth and scope of the farm. Impressive, to say the least. The two main permanent structures had loading docks, and a large, refrigerated truck was pulling away from the one to the left. Both buildings were painted sea-foam green with island murals on the front and meticulous landscaping all around.

"This is quite a setup," I commented to Joe Earl as we

climbed out of the truck. I pointed at the "Office" sign on one of the main buildings, and we headed in that direction. Two elderly guys in overalls, carrying pipe parts and nets, shuffled past us silently, both of them on the high side of seventy.

"Buenos dias," one of them said with a half-smile.

I smiled back. "Do you work here?"

They didn't stop or respond.

I opened my mouth to repeat my question, but was interrupted by a familiar voice. "Hi y'all. Can I help you?"

Travis Harper came toward us, but there were no overalls on him, thank you very much. He sported khaki chinos, short-sleeved, white polo shirt, and a straw, Panama hat. Ever the southern gentleman, right down to the polished, leather loafers. The elderly men disappeared around the corner of the building, but I sensed their continued scrutiny.

Not sure what that was all about, I murmured to Joe Earl, "Do you speak Spanish?"

"Un poco."

"Good. See what you can find out from them." I stretched my hand out in Travis's direction. "Hi, Mr. Harper. I'm Mallie Monroe, Senior Reporter for the *Observer,* and this is my assistant, Joe Earl." Joe Earl waved his iPhone as a greeting. "I'm doing a story on Bucky McGuire's death."

"You're the young woman from the town-hall meeting," Travis cut in, a brief, calculating gleam darting across his eyes. Just a momentary blip, but I caught it.

"Guilty." I shook his hand. "I was there as part of my local-politics beat, expecting the usual routine session, but it turned out to be quite a melee with that fish fight. Did you ever get the tilapia guts off your jacket?"

"No." His features tightened.

"And I'm sure you heard about Bucky's death only hours afterwards."

"Yes." More tightening of the face.

"Very sad and . . . unexpected." Clearing my throat, I looked away with a shake of my head. "It's hard to believe that someone who appeared to be the picture of good health just keeled over like that in a fish tank."

"Was there something odd about Bucky's demise?" he asked.

I lifted my shoulders in feigned ignorance.

"If there was, the police probably need to arrest that maniac, Wanda Sue. I don't need to remind you that she threatened all of us with a gun."

"Flare gun," I corrected. "And, no, to my knowledge, the police haven't released a statement, nor has she been arrested." Hitching my hobo bag higher on my shoulder, I continued in a neutral voice, "Not to be disrespectful, but *you* were the one pummeling Bucky with fish guts on the floor only hours before he died. If there was foul play, I might be wrong, but you could be considered a person of interest."

A red flush of anger burned across his face, but he recovered quickly with a charming smile that didn't quite meet his eyes. "Where are my manners? Here I am keeping you standing under the hot sun when we could be cool and comfortable inside my office. Come on in. I've got a fresh batch of iced coffee and homemade, Florida-orange cake."

Coffee? Cake? My heartbeat quickened at the holy grail of caffeine and sugar. I wasn't a big fan of the "iced" part, but I'd take my java any way I could get it. "Lead the way."

"Um . . . I'm going to look around the property, if you don't mind, Mr. Harper," Joe Earl cut in. "I'm really interested in tilapia farming."

Travis hesitated for a fraction of a minute. "Sure, young fella, but don't take any pictures of the tanks and facilities. My workers don't like to be photographed."

Joe Earl moved off toward one of the large, canvas-covered

structures that housed the fish tanks.

"Now, Molly—"

"Mallie," I corrected, as I followed him into the office.

"My apologies, my dear. *Mallie.* Lovely name and so distinctive." He removed his straw hat, placing it carefully on an antique, wooden rack next to the door. "I'll get us some coffee and then we can chat." He gestured toward a sofa and coffee table off to one side of the room. "Cream? Sugar?"

"Black, please." I took in the surroundings as I headed for the sitting area, my sneakers squeaking on the wood floor. Travis had obviously taken great pains to give the office a homey yet refined feel, from the warm-yellow walls to the cozy, overstuffed furniture and subtle smell of cinnamon potpourri. It screamed southern charm, rather than fish farmer.

As I sat down on the red and yellow, tropical-patterned sofa, I inhaled the mouth-watering aroma of baked goods as Travis returned with our refreshments. Maybe there *was* something to this southern hospitality after all—even during a murder investigation. I could get my caffeine and sugar fix along with an interview all at the same time.

"Here we are." He set down a tray with delicate, etched glasses filled with ice, a silver coffee pot, and paper-thin cake slices. Then, he seated himself in a wingback chair and slowly poured a small amount of coffee over the ice. "The trick is to let the coffee cool before you fill the glasses. Too hot and they shatter."

"I'll remember that." *Hah.* My glow of satisfaction faded at the miniscule portions of the confection and half glass of my favorite adult beverage.

Helping myself to the cake, it started to break apart, so I quickly gobbled it up. Not wanting to look too eager for more, I took a few sips of coffee and reminded myself that Senior

Reporters didn't indulge in those weaknesses. They were tough as nails.

And I figured I could always swing into the Dairy Queen for an ice-cream cone dipped in chocolate on the way back to the office.

"How long have you known Bucky McGuire?" I asked, as I grabbed my notepad and pen from my bag. "You were partners at one time, but how far back did your acquaintance go?"

Travis leaned back in his chair, taking a long drink before he answered. "Let me see. I guess that I've known him maybe ten years or so, from when I first came to Coral Island. He did some landscaping for me at my house." He crossed his legs, smoothing down the neatly pressed material of his trousers in a relaxed gesture. But I still detected a certain wariness around the eyes every time his glance darted back to me. Could it be just nervousness, or did he have something to hide?

"When did the two of you start the tilapia farm?"

"Uh . . . about . . . maybe five years ago," he said slowly, as if running through a mental calendar. "I provided the business expertise for Tropical Tilapia, and Bucky oversaw all day-to-day aspects related to the fish production—the water quality, breeding—and the fertilizer/landscaping, of course."

"Sounds like a match made in heaven," I said, jotting down some notes and gulping the rest of my coffee in one swallow. Maybe he'd take pity on me and refill the glass. "So what caused the rift? Why did you break up the partnership?"

"Everything was great in the beginning, but then . . ." He stared off in the distance for a few moments and sighed deeply. "I don't wish to speak ill of the dead, but I discovered that Bucky wasn't exactly . . . well, how should I say it? Not the most ethical person in terms of bookkeeping."

"You mean he stole from you?" I stopped writing.

"Let's just say my profits were dwindling every quarter, even though our business was thriving. There was no apparent reason for the financial downturn. Of course, I never accused him of anything. A gentleman would never do that. I simply said that I wanted to take the company in a new direction, and he was more than willing to let me buy him out. In fact, he still did landscaping work here."

"So you parted ways amicably?"

"Very much so." He held up the silver pot and refilled my glass.

"That's interesting, because it seemed to me at the town-hall meeting like there was bad blood between the two of you, what with the personal attacks and the fish fight." I pretended to jot down a few notes again.

He set his glass on the table with a distinct thud, but he kept his composure. "Look here, you think I had a problem with my ex-partner? Maybe I did at one time, but I'd moved on. That's what professionals do. We take care of business. You're way off base if you think I had an ax to grind with Bucky McGuire."

"But at the town-council meeting—"

"You didn't take that seriously, did you? That was just pure political show. Nothing else."

"Oh." *And pigs fly.*

"I don't have to remind you that Wanda Sue was practically unhinged when it came to Bucky McGuire. She couldn't forget that he left her for another woman. In fact, I remember when they were dating—Bucky was still my partner—all they did was fight. One time, she hit him upside of the head with a frying pan. Crazier than a road lizard." His southern drawl became more pronounced as he grew animated.

I guess the whole island knew about the frying-pan incident. "Did you know that Bucky was engaged to Destiny Ransford?" I asked, helping myself to the refreshed glass of iced coffee. "I interviewed her a little while ago, and she said that they intended to get married next year." Like my plans with Cole—if I ever found the diamond ring again.

Travis didn't blink. "I was aware that they had a relationship, but I didn't know they intended to get married."

"Were you in love with Destiny?"

"Ms. Monroe, I'm on the Shoreline Bank Board of Directors. Our relationship is purely professional." Travis's eyes narrowed as he rose to his feet. "I've been quite patient with your probing, but this interview is over. I told you everything I know: Bucky was my partner, and, if there was foul play involved in his death, the police need to arrest Wanda Sue. That's all I have to say."

I flipped my notepad shut, knowing that I wouldn't get anything else today. "Thanks for your time, and please call me if you have any more information." I set my card on the silver tray. As I started for the door, one of the aging workers flung it open. *"Fuego! Fuego!"*

Even I knew what that meant: *Fire.*

Chapter Nine

"Damn. They're at it again!" Travis proclaimed in a loud voice as he dashed out the front door, the workman following him with a little bounce to his hobbling gait. If I didn't know better (and I didn't), I'd swear I spied a little wink from the geriatric employee.

"I won't stand for this anymore! I've *had* it," Travis's voice took on a tinge of righteous indignation as it faded in the distance.

Joe Earl then appeared in the doorway.

"What's going on?" I asked, retrieving my coat.

"You'll see."

I looked around for a telltale sign of smoke and noticed a man heading to the parking lot. His back was to us, but I thought I detected a familiar silver ponytail and doo-rag. Coop? What was he doing here?

I shouted his name and started off in that direction.

"No, not that way." Joe Earl caught my arm. "Let's go out the back door."

"But I think I saw—"

"Just trust me." Joe Earl hustled me toward the back door.

"It says emergency exit," I protested as he kept propelling me. He pushed open the door and we tumbled outside into the warm air that smelled . . . sooty. "Jeez, is there a brushfire? We'd better call the fire department." I reached for my cell phone.

"No, it's not a brush fire. That one old codger likes to burn garbage in the trash can, and it ignited into a full-fledged bonfire. I got the feeling they burn trash just to irritate Travis. But I thought I'd use the diversion, so I could show you what's going on. Follow me." He took off toward one of the large, covered frame structures.

I started running after him, my bag swinging behind me. "What? Where are we going? Joe Earl, stop!"

He kept jogging, so I had no choice but to follow in pursuit—sort of. My fast-food, long-hours-at-the-newspaper lifestyle didn't exactly lend itself to sprinting without blowing out a lung. So, I managed a short trot, then loped like a lame horse to try and keep up with him. But I kept falling farther behind, my breath coming in jagged gasps, and my heart pounding.

"Wait up!" I cried out, not sure if I might need a 9-1-1 call myself if I kept this pace up (which had slowed down to a skip). I really needed to get back into Tae Kwon Do class.

"Almost there!" Joe Earl waved me on.

Lungs ready to burst, I scuttled the last few yards until we entered the tent. Leaning on a wooden post, I bent over, wheezing to catch my breath. "This had better be good. I almost collapsed back there." Chest heaving, I straightened slowly.

"Oh, it's worth it." He strode down the aisle between the large tilapia tanks, one of them with red fish on the right and the other with white fish on the left.

Then, I caught a whiff of decaying carcasses. Pungent didn't even begin to describe the aquatic version of roadkill. "What the hell is that stench?"

Joe Earl grabbed a net and skimmed the water, catching a few slow-moving tilapia. "From what I read on the Internet about the fish-farming process, there appears to be something wrong with the filtration system in all of the tanks. It's killing the fish. If they don't have clean water, they get lethargic and die."

I leaned over the tank and took a short breath, then immediately turned my head away with a gasp. "They smell like they're one fin away from that big tilapia tank in the sky."

He turned the net over, spilling the fish back into the tank. They didn't swim off but, rather, floated for a few seconds then drifted away with a tiny movement of their tails.

"You don't think he's *selling* these fish, do you?" I stepped back from the tank.

"Dunno. But it's a given that nobody has been attending these tanks for a few weeks." Joe Earl replaced the fish net in the corner. "Those two oldies, Jose and Pepe, told me they're the only two workers left out of the twelve guys that used to monitor the tanks."

"Travis fired all of his crew?"

"Looks like it. Travis told Jose and Pepe he was going to rehire someone to help out, but they didn't believe him."

"But that doesn't make sense."

"Unless the dude is having cash-flow problems, none of this neglect makes any sense," Joe Earl pointed out. "That would be the only reason to cut his workmen to a skeleton crew and allow the fish tanks to turn into these cesspools."

"Poor fish," I murmured, taking another glance at the barely-moving tilapia. "We definitely need a financial report on Travis's business."

"As soon as I can—"

"Ms. Monroe!" Travis was shouting from somewhere outside.

My eyes met Joe Earl's with some alarm. "We can't let him find us in here," I whispered, gesturing at the back of the large tent.

We hurried out, circled around the canvas structure, and met Travis out front. He was moving fast to intercept us.

"Oh, sorry, we got lost—" I began in a suitably apologetic tone.

"Were you in that tent?" Streaks of soot crisscrossed his face and shirt.

"We didn't have the chance." I shrugged. "What happened with the fire? Is it a big blaze? Are we in any danger?"

"No and no. Some of my idiotic workers lit up paper inside a trash can," Travis said in a short, clipped voice, wiping his face with a white handkerchief. "It's contained now."

"Thank goodness. The last thing you need is a brushfire around here now that the rainy season is over." I grabbed Joe Earl's arm. "Well, we've got to get going. Thanks again for the interview."

Travis didn't move, blocking our path to my truck. "My workmen told me this young fella asked a lot of questions and was nosing around my property." He leveled a severe glance at Joe Earl. "Is that true?"

"Define 'nosing,' " Joe Earl challenged.

Travis wiped his forehead with an impatient swipe. "I think it's best if the two of you hit the road and don't come back."

"You did give us permission to look around," I reminded him.

"That's the only reason I'm not calling the police to have you both arrested."

Joe Earl straightened, standing eye level with Travis. "Hey, man, I wasn't doing anything wrong. If you've got nothing to hide, you shouldn't mind people checking out your operation."

Travis's eyes narrowed. "How dare you."

"I can assure you that Joe Earl wasn't snooping." I edged around Travis, trying to tug Joe Earl behind me. The last thing I needed was a replay of a Travis/Bucky fight, with Joe Earl as the new and improved Bucky. I didn't want any trouble, and I especially didn't want to jeopardize the status of my assistant who could make coffee, do research on his iPhone in a flash, and talk to a haunted violin (maybe I could do without the last item). "Come on, Joe Earl."

He remained rooted in place.

After a few moments, he gave in and let me lead him toward Rusty. "What's wrong with you?" I muttered under my breath.

"That dude was staring me down. I couldn't let him get the upper hand."

"Spare me the macho head games," I cut in swiftly. "If Travis was involved in Bucky's death, the last thing we want to do is tick him off. I don't want to end *my* days belly up in a fish tank." Certainly not before my wedding.

Joe Earl flexed his nonexistent muscles. "I could take him on any day of the week."

"Oh, pleeeeease." I glanced over my shoulder and spied Travis still watching us. Suddenly nervous, I slid into Rusty, then leaned over and opened the passenger door. "Get in. Now."

Joe Earl complied, taking his time to slide into the truck. As soon as Mr. Machismo settled into his seat, I cranked up the engine and revved out of the parking lot, causing Rusty to thump violently on the unpaved road. "I want to put as much distance between Travis and us as possible."

"He bullies those two old workmen, and I don't believe for one minute that they ratted me out. They hate Travis and think he's going to fire them any day."

"Take it easy."

"I hate bullies." He clutched the armrest as Rusty lurched down the road. "They can make your life a living hell, and I should know. As a computer nerd without a dad, I was fair game for every jerkface high-school guy going."

Glancing at him briefly, I saw his knuckles had turned almost white. "Where was your father?"

"Just took off years ago." Joe Earl shrugged. "I was going to ask the Abe Lincoln violin, but it didn't seem worth the effort."

"I agree." My truck hit a large pothole and shuddered like

the *Titanic* when it hit the iceberg. I let up on the gas pedal. "All the more reason to find out what's going on at that tilapia farm, if only to stop Travis's exploitation of his workers." I held the steering wheel tightly as we drove in silence for a few minutes. Obviously, there was more to Joe Earl than met the eye. "I didn't get much out of Travis, except that Bucky was supposedly embezzling money from him. Not sure I believe that. And I couldn't quite pinpoint what his connection is with Destiny, aside from the fact he's on the board of her bank." My battered truck lurched and chugged over the potholes until we emerged onto Cypress Road. Once we hit paved road again, I exhaled in relief and relaxed my death grip on the steering wheel. "Tell me more about the fish tanks."

"They're definitely being neglected and, from what I read online, it's not that difficult to keep the water fresh." Joe Earl relaxed again and propped his arm against the passenger door. "While I check into his finances, we need someone to nose around the tilapia farm—a person whom Travis wouldn't suspect of being a spy. Like an undercover mole."

I nodded. "The problem is, Travis struck me as a pretty suspicious kind of guy. We'd have to find an expert snoop, trained in the art of deception."

"All of his workmen look like they're over seventy, at least," Joe Earl interjected. "I don't think they're going to be much help."

I stared at the road before me, an idea slowly taking form as I headed back to the *Observer* office. "That's not going to be a problem."

It was mad.

It was crazy.

And it just might work.

★ ★ ★ ★ ★

An hour later, we sat at Anita's conference table behind the taped window, formulating a plan with our geriatric Snoop Dog Extraordinaire: Pop Pop Welch. Okay, call me wacko, but that old man had some untapped depth underneath the wrinkles and free-floating dentures. Besides, he was the only person over seventy that I knew who might be game enough to give fish espionage a try.

"Now, Pop Pop, all you have to do is show up at Tropical Tilapia and ask Travis if he's looking for any workers."

"Should I wear a disguise?" Pop Pop stroked his thinning hair and adjusted his thick bifocals. "I could shave off about ten years with a toupee and contacts."

I blinked, trying not to summon an image of Pop Pop with a hair rug. Best not to go there.

"You just need to look like yourself," I assured him. "Travis likes . . . uh . . . mature workmen."

"Go ahead and say it, missy. He likes to hire oldies like me. People think 'cause I'm on Medicare that I don't know the score. These guys like Travis always think they can pay us seniors low wages and work us to death. But I wasn't born yesterday." He thumped his chest, then took a whiff of oxygen. "No sir-reee."

"I promise that the *Observer* will reimburse you appropriately for your time," I explained, making an executive decision in Anita's absence and praying she would follow through.

"Deal." Pop Pop spat in his hand and held it out.

Waving aside the "spittle shake," I continued, "We need to know why the tilapia are dying. So poke around the fish tanks and see what's going on. Keep your eyes open to anything that seems a little unusual or out of the ordinary. I'll give you more information down the road, but first, we need to know what's going on here."

Pop Pop nodded knowingly. "An expose on a fish killer?"

"Sort of." I cleared my throat. "Suffice it to say, I need some firsthand, reliable information on the ground from a source that I can trust—you. I'm counting on you, Pop Pop. You know how important it is for us to shine a light in the darkness. That's how Anita puts it. Journalists have to be fearless." My motor mouth had kicked in big-time with excitement.

My Senior Reporter status was going to my head.

"Count me in." Pop Pop gave a thumbs-up, then started coughing until he took another whiff of oxygen.

Uh-oh.

"Maybe this isn't such a good idea," I murmured to Joe Earl as I slapped Pop Pop on the back. "I don't want anything to happen to him."

"I can take care of myself, missy," Pop Pop chimed in as he got control of his wheezing. "Especially now I've got my new hearing aids. I'll hear everything that's going on at that fish farm, trust me." He tapped his ears with a grin. "Nothing will get past these top-of-the-line Bellsound Bolds."

"Are they new?" I tried to peer at his ears.

"No, they're not *blue,*" he scoffed.

Doubts flooded through me with the rushing force of a train. Maybe I'd gotten too carried away. "You've got your cell phone don't you, Pop Pop?"

"Right here." He held up a slide-style model. "I've got you on speed dial from our dating days."

"We were *not* dating," I retorted

Joe Earl kicked me under the table.

"Okay, we went out a few times, but it was strictly newspaper business," I corrected myself.

Joe Earl kicked me again.

"All right, we're good friends."

My Geritol-set handyman broke into a wide smile.

"Pop Pop, if anything seems off, or if you feel the slightest sense of danger at the tilapia farm, I want you to get out of there pronto," I said, still worried about him. "Call in every two hours, so I know you're okay."

"See?" Pop Pop transferred his gaze in Joe Earl's direction with a click of his tongue. "She can't stand to have me out of her sight even for a short time."

"That's not exactly true." Still, I couldn't resist giving him a hug. What can I say? The never-give-in gumption at his age was inspiring.

"I'm ready to roll." Pop Pop wheeled back his oxygen tank and it hit the already-cracked window. The glass gave way and shattered all over the floor.

Not a good sign.

An hour later, the repairman had returned, removed Anita's cubicle window, and installed a temporary privacy barrier, which consisted of a piece of cardboard taped to the cubicle wall. After raiding the petty-cash jar for a tip, I ushered him out of the office.

Joe Earl tapped the cardboard. "I like it better than the glass."

"At least when Anita gets back, we won't have to see her sitting there."

"Sounds like a plus." He heaved his backpack over his shoulder.

Major plus, indeed. "But I hope breaking a window doesn't bring seven years of bad luck like it does with a mirror." I found a stray bit of glass as we strolled toward the front door.

Joe Earl kicked a few additional shards out of his way. "You need to bury a couple of pieces of the glass during the full moon. I heard it wipes out any bad luck."

"I'd rather hang garlic around my neck."

"Suit yourself." He gave me a little salute and headed out.

I paused, then pocketed a small piece of glass for a beach burial at the Twin Palms. It couldn't hurt.

On the way back to my desk, my cell phone began to ring. I checked the name and squealed, "Sandy!"

"Hi, Mallie," her cheery voice greeted me. "How's it going?"

I took in a deep breath. "So-so in terms of getting the edition out, but I've got Joe Earl working here as my assistant."

"On payroll?"

"Maybe."

Sandy started chuckling. "I can hardly wait to hear what Anita thinks about that one." A jumble of voices in the background started up. "Jimmy and I are sightseeing at the Fountain of Youth Archeological Park. It's supposed to be the spot where Ponce de Leon found a spring with the secret of eternal youth."

"Did you take a drink of the magic water?" I could use a swig from the fountain myself right now.

"Not exactly." She lowered her tone to a whisper. "The spring is more like a trickle over some dirty rocks. I didn't want to go near it." She said something else, but I couldn't make it out because of the background noise growing louder. "Sorry, Mallie, but there's a crowd gathering for the cannon demo."

"My favorite part," Jimmy exclaimed into the phone. "We saw it yesterday and came back for more."

"Then I'd better get in everything that's been going on here fast." I took a deep breath and cranked up the Mallie Motor Mouth for a marathon race, covering everything from the town-council meeting to Wanda Sue firing a flare gun, to Bucky McGuire's death in less than a three-minute verbal mile.

"Did you say Bucky McGuire might've been killed?" she exclaimed, and the voices on her end turned silent.

"It's possible. He went down in the fish tank at the town hall from a blow to the back of his head, but I can't tell anybody else that except our newspaper staff." I paused and paced around the empty office, cell phone plastered to my ear. "The last part is kind of lame: I've had to enlist Pop Pop to go undercover at the Tropical Tilapia farm to check out a lead—"

"*What?*"

" 'Fraid so."

"On payroll?"

"Guess so." I slumped into my desk chair. "I had no choice. My front-page story depends on it. It's only two days away from the *Observer* deadline, and I need more info about what might've led to Bucky's demise."

"You're turning into Anita! Next thing, you'll be raiding old folks' homes for freelancers." The cannon fired on Sandy's end with a loud boom. I snapped the phone shut and threw it down.

Me? Anita?

Never.

Ever.

"I am *not* my crusty, conniving boss. I'm just trying to get a job done," I pronounced to the empty office, then I proceeded to buckle down with renewed vigor on this week's edition to distract myself. I couldn't contemplate the implications of becoming an Anita clone just because I asked my geriatric handyman for help. What did Sandy know, anyway? She was a newlywed with her perceptions altered by a love-drenched, cannon-shelled honeymoon.

After working on the layout for two hours, I had a decent mock-up between the local events, community meetings, and letters to the editor. Nothing earthshaking, but at least enough to fill the back pages. I left the above-the-fold headline blank, though I sketched out the story on Bucky's death that I could edit the next morning. I said a quick prayer for inspiration to finish the story to St. Paul, patron saint of journalists, then added a quickie to Michael, Gabriel, and Raphael, the worker-bee angels of communication, that I wouldn't lose my temporary reporters (and I use that term loosely).

Front page, below the fold, would have to be the bicycle-bandit story or the Abe Lincoln violin feature.

Just then, my cell phone dinged. Thinking it might be a message from Pop Pop, I snatched it off my desk with lightning speed.

But it wasn't him.

Tagline: Liz Ellis.

Mallie: If you want to interview me about the plant killer, I might reconsider—if I receive a formal apology from you about the harassment outside the bank today.

Otherwise I'll have no choice, other than to proceed with my lawsuit.

You Know Who—Liz.

Groaning, I e-mailed her back. "I'll call you."

Okay, I didn't want to interview her, or be within twenty miles of the woman, for that matter. But I also didn't relish having to tell Anita on her first day back that someone was suing the paper—and me.

I sighed.

"Hard day?"

Raising my head, I savored the image of Nick Billie leaning against the front doorframe with his arms crossed against his chest.

"You have no idea," I mumbled. Though it just got a little better.

"Let me see if I can take a guess. You're still desperately trying to get a front-page story, Pop Pop caused a ruckus at the Island Diner and sent an old lady to the ER, and then you badgered Travis about Bucky's death to the point he called me and complained that you were harassing him." He paused with one raised brow. "Am I tracking the day's misadventures?"

"Like a NASCAR racer." I leaned back in my chair and smiled, deciding that he did *not* need to know about Pop Pop's recent assignment. "Who would've thought being in charge would be such a hassle? I never thought I'd say this, but I'm starting to sympathize with Anita and her mean-assed ways. Getting out the newspaper every week is such a huge responsibility, no matter who is here to help. Of course, all I've got is Madame Geri and her haunted violin and Bernice with her bicycle bandit."

"Sorry to make your day worse, but I think we caught the thief." He walked in my direction, causing my heart to beat a little faster.

I immediately straightened, causing the recently fixed wooden chair—and me—to tip forward.

Nick instantly was there, catching the arms of my chair to steady it. As I straightened and flipped my curls back, his face was inches from mine.

"Who . . . did it? I mean, who's the bandit?" My mouth had turned dry as a piece of cotton.

His face moved closer. "Just some high-school kid who was playing pranks on his neighbors."

Damn. "No above-the-fold, front-page story there."

"Nope."

I could feel the movement of his breathing, heavy and warm. "My deadline is . . . looming and that leaves me the Abe Lincoln violin."

"Guess so."

He touched his mouth to mine, a mere brush, tantalizing me to push it further.

Could I? Should I give in?

Oscar Wilde's delightfully naughty quote flitted through my mind: *The only way to get rid of temptation is to yield to it.*

At the last minute, I pulled back and squared my shoulders

with determined resolve. *Oscar Wilde be damned. Everyone knows he ended up in prison.* Meeting Nick's gaze directly, I stammered, "I . . . thought things were over between us."

"Not by a long shot." He dropped a short, hard kiss on my lips. "My head says to walk away, but my heart won't let me."

"Just give me a little time."

He didn't respond for a few long moments, then stepped back and sat on the corner of my desk. "Fair enough. Just don't take too long, okay?"

I stretched out my hand. "It's a deal." We shook on it, and he held my hand a little longer than necessary, but I didn't protest. "Not to be all business again, but can you give me the latest scoop on Bucky's case?"

"What did Destiny and Travis tell you?" he countered.

"You first," I prompted, picking up my notebook and pen. Anita would be proud.

"We found a possible murder weapon, for the record."

"Already?" I said, barely able to control my gasp of surprise.

"My deputies have been searching outside the town hall the last twenty-four hours, and they turned up something interesting. We're doing the testing now to see if the blood type matches Bucky's, and if the object conforms to the wound."

I was scribbling madly. "When will you know for sure?"

"A couple of days."

"Oh, come on. You can fast-track those results. Don't hold out on me now, Nick." I fastened a pleading glance on him, eyes wide and hopeful.

He fiddled with his silver and turquoise belt buckle. "Maybe I'll have something in twenty-four hours, but I can't guarantee it."

"Fair enough."

He still didn't look up, and I sensed his reluctance held something else that I didn't want to hear. "What are you *not* telling me?"

"I gave you my *official* update."

Raising my brows, I continued, "Off the record?"

He shoved a hand through his straight, black hair, his face taking on a pained expression. "The possible weapon is . . . a frying pan."

I dropped my pen.

Chapter Ten

"Whoa. Time out." I made the T motion with my hands. "You're not suggesting that Wanda Sue—"

"I haven't given you any information for the record beyond the fact that we might've found a possible murder weapon. That's it."

"And you're certain there was blood on it?"

He nodded.

"Va Fa Napoli!"

"Huh?"

"It's a sanitized curse from Joey on *Friends.* I must've fallen sleep with the TV on a repeat last night and flashed back in shock." I was babbling, but nothing concrete surfaced as my mind raced about looking for reasons why a bloody frying pan was found near the town hall. "Maybe that guy who cooks for the town-hall chicken dinners cut his hand while he was stir-frying. He's got arthritis pretty bad and could've lost his grip."

"Unlikely. The blood was on the base of the pan, not the handle." His features shuttered down, and the window of our connection closed. Now it was all business between us, and he was back to the island cop and I was back to the *Observer* Senior Reporter.

But I couldn't pretend to be an objective journalist; this was Wanda Sue's life at stake.

Nick pushed himself upright again. "Mallie, I've got no choice; I have to bring Wanda Sue in for questioning."

"Don't you think the frying pan turning up outside the town hall is just a bit too convenient? Everyone on the island knew that Wanda Sue threatened Bucky with a frying pan when their relationship had soured, so to think that she decided to kill him with the same type of weapon is just plain caca." I stood up, as well. "It's a frame."

"I don't like it either, but she's now a person of interest."

I bit my lip and shook my head.

"I'm sorry, Mallie." He started to say something else, but apparently thought better of it, and left without another word.

My mind blanked out for a few moments in an empty, gray space as I tried to take in the fact that my oldest and dearest island BFF might be arrested for murder.

No way would I let that happen. I couldn't. And as a Senior Reporter, I had my share of resources.

First, I had to redeploy my crackerjack team with our new objective: find Bucky's killer to clear Wanda Sue. Grabbing my cell phone, I called Bernice, left her a message about the bicycle-bandit's arrest, and asked her to come in tomorrow morning to help with this investigative story instead. Maybe she could tail Destiny Ransford; there was more to Miss-Grieving-Bank-Manager than met the eye.

After that, I called Madame Geri, who picked up on the first ring. "Wanda Sue is in deep trouble, isn't she?" said Madame Geri.

"Up to her neck." That damned spirit world was faster than the speed of light. "Put the Abe Lincoln-violin piece on the back burner. I need help on the Bucky McGuire story. I've got someone watching Travis, and I'm going to ask Bernice to follow Destiny. I want you to get with Joe Earl—he's already checking into Travis's finances—and see what the two of you can find out about Liz Ellis. She's one of Bucky's disgruntled customers."

"Will do. The Abe story is almost finished, but tip number four from the *Dummy's Guide* says to be flexible. I'm on board."

"Thanks."

"One last thing. I keep getting the image of an omelet skillet as the murder weapon."

"Frying pan. Off the record."

"Ouch." Madame Geri clicked off.

I texted Joe Earl with his additional assignment and then speed dialed Pop Pop. After about a dozen rings and no voice mail, I was ready to forget it when he finally picked up.

"Pop Pop, did you get hired?" I asked in a loud voice, hoping he could hear me.

"No need to shout, missy. I've got my hearing aids on high volume." He coughed a few times and inhaled audibly (I presumed he had the oxygen tank nearby). "I aced the interview. You're now talking to Mr. Travis's new Fish Operations Foreman."

"Perfect!"

"Easy breezy, for those of us who know how to present ourselves in an interview." He lowered his voice. "And I can already tell there's something rotten going on here."

"Fish killing?"

"Worse. I've been talking with Jose and Pepe and found out Travis is paying them less than minimum wage. He calls it the gray-hair scale. Can you believe it? I can't let my fellow seniors be exploited like that."

"Pop Pop, I need you to stay focused on your assignment: gleaning information about the tilapia farm."

"I am, but first I've got to take care of the elder abuse going on here."

My fingers tightened around the phone. "I repeat—*stay focused.* I'm on a tight deadline here with my edition."

"Ten-four, missy." Pop Pop cackled. "Listen, here's what I

intend to do. I'm going to unionize the workers. Jose, Pepe, and I are going to form the United Tilapia Farm Workers. Senior brothers unite!"

"What?"

"Don't worry, Mallie, it won't take long to file the paperwork, and I can nose around the fish tanks at the same time. I already called someone with the AFL-CIO."

I hung up. Okay, that one was turning out to be a bust. Luckily, I still had Bernice, Joe Earl, and Madame Geri.

"Coming through!" a familiar voice sang out. I ran to the open office area just in time to see Bernice whirling through the door on a unicycle with tiny training wheels. "Hey, Mallie, thanks for the call about the bike bandit, but I already knew it. I was there when Nick and his deputy lectured that neighbor kid for stealing bicycles, and he had quite a stockpile of purloined bikes, let me tell you. Anyway, no one was pressing charges, so he didn't get arrested, just community service. Sad that it turned out to be a ho-hum kind of story after all." She gave a faux yawn. "But lookee what I found at his house."

My eyes widened as I spied about six inches of latex-encased, droopy buttocks on either side of the seat, precariously balanced over a single, thin tire. Bernice slowed down as she took the corner around my desk. "Nick couldn't fit all the stolen bikes in his truck, so he said I could take the unicycle to the police station. Cool, huh? I couldn't resist popping it out of my car for a little tour around the newspaper office to show you." She backpedaled and twirled to the right, then left.

I had to admit that her sense of balance seemed impressive.

Then she spun the wheel in a circle and aimed for the back of the office.

"All right, that's enough," I ordered. "Get off that thing. You're heading right for the coffeepot!"

She jerked her right foot down but didn't slow down. "Damn

that little weasel thief. The brakes don't work. I can't stop." A stream of expletives emitted from her until the unicycle rammed into the small table, causing Bernice to flip over and—even worse—take the coffeepot with her.

The glass carafe shattered upon impact.

"I broke my arm," Bernice shouted. By the time I got over to her, she was on the floor, clutching her right elbow and kicking the bike tire. "Call 9-1-1, you dummy."

Great.

Now I was down to Joe Earl and Madame Geri.

After calling the paramedics for the second time in two days, waving Bernice off to the ER (she grumbled the entire time about having broken her "fighting arm," whatever that meant), and mourning my coffee pot, I finally climbed, exhausted and weary, into my truck and headed out.

Well . . . maybe I'd taken one more peek in my desk drawer for the diamond engagement ring. Still nada.

As I slowly drove along Cypress Drive, I found myself staring at the road with a numb, almost unseeing gaze. Between Wanda Sue's woes and this whole editor thing, I was ready for Anita to return. Okay. I'd admitted it. It was time for her to come back and pick up the reins again, so I could take a vacation. In the meantime, I needed a heavy-duty dose of clear-my-head, forget-about-the-world zone-out in my Airstream.

When I reached the Twin Palms RV Park, my mouth spread into a tired, but happy smile. The sight of the sturdy trailers, RVs, and fifth-wheels lined up along the small strip of sand had a lovely, secure feel. *Home.* I parked my truck, then glanced at Cole's van—dark and quiet—and my neighbor on the other side—outside lights on, with the song "Love, Love, Love" playing from a boom box.

Was Lenny Kravitz next door?

Who cared at this point?

Stumbling out of Rusty, I yawned and stretched my arms overhead.

"Miss Mallie?" a voice said from behind.

Startled, I spun around to see Coop standing under my awning in jeans with a splashy, tropical shirt and black, cotton doo-rag. Evening garb.

"I saw you at the Tropical Tilapia today and remembered you said to call if I had any information about Bucky." He held out my business card. "I forgot to pin the number to my shirt, but found the card right here when I was going to do my laundry this morning." He tapped his shirt pocket. "I called the newspaper earlier today—at least I think I did—and some woman named Jerry told me you lived at the Twin Palms."

"Madame Geri. She's the island freelance psychic who writes our Astrology Now! column." Nice to know that she's just handing out my home address to anyone who calls the *Observer.* No raise for her—one year.

His features crumpled into a puzzled frown. "I don't remember any psychic stuff, but then again that memory thing makes it hard for me to recall . . ." He spread his hands in helpless appeal.

"Do you want to sit down?" I gestured toward my picnic table and pulled my sweater tighter. Though my Airstream blocked the wind coming in off the Gulf, the temperature was dropping fast, and all I had on under the sweater was a thin, cotton t-shirt.

"Nah, I think I'll stand." He shifted from one foot to the other, rubbing his hands together.

"Okay." Why was he so nervous?

My awning flapped in the breeze, and the tide rolled in with a soft, rhythmic swell.

I waited, detecting Kong's scratching the inside of the

Airstream door. He wouldn't be able to wait much longer to take a business break. "I hate to sound impatient, but I'm going to need to walk my dog in a minute. What's up?"

He placed his hands on his waist and drew in a deep breath and let it out slowly (very slowly). "I'm not sure if this means anything or not, 'cause I'm still in shock about Bucky. And I'm a loyal employee, as I told you."

"I don't think anyone would question that." Kong's scratching grew louder. "Is it connected to the tilapia farm?"

"Sort of."

Kong gave a little yelp.

"And Travis Harper?"

"Yep."

"Could you be a little more specific?" Shivering, I realized that I was now officially doing twenty questions outside my Airstream in a blustering wind with a desperate dog inside. A Senior Reporter would know how to elicit the info a little faster, even with a guy who had a questionable memory.

"All right." He stopped wringing his hands. "For the last couple of months, I'd go to Tropical Tilapia two or three times a week to trim bushes, pull weeds—the usual kind of landscaping work that Bucky and I did for Travis. But a little while ago, I got the sense that Travis was watching me."

My interest perked up in spite of Kong's persistent barks. "What do you mean?"

"I can't say that I remember it exactly, but I think I caught him nosing around my truck."

"Did he take anything?"

"Not sure."

Of course.

"It was more of a feeling than a fact," he said, jamming his hands in his jeans pockets. "Something just felt off. In fact, I didn't like going there after Travis fired everyone except Jose and Pepe. The place felt . . . sad."

"I sensed that, too." I folded my arms over my chest, trying to ignore the chill as I digested Coop's information. "Did Bucky ever tell you about his falling out with Travis?"

"Not that I can recollect." He hunched his shoulders with a shake of his head. "When they dissolved their partnership, I stayed working for Bucky since he'd hired me in the first place to do landscaping work. The fish-farm workers stayed with Travis."

"The few who are left."

"Yeah. Pepe and Jose are worried that they won't have a job by the end of the year. It's a terrible thing to be unemployed so late in life."

I nodded. "Do you think Travis's downsizing his crew has anything to do with his cagey behavior? I mean, was he trying to hide something from you?"

"Possibly. He sure didn't like me talking to Pepe and Jose. Never let the two of them talk to me alone. But I caught snatches of their conversation about the '*un jefe horrible.*' Horrible boss." Coop smiled. "I picked up a little Spanish from them."

At the very least, Travis was a rigid, tightfisted boss. Oh, wait. All that meant was he could be Anita's fraternal twin and they shared the cheap gene.

Coop scratched his doo-rag. "I'm going to search through all my shirt pockets in case I stashed any other notes that I forgot. I have a huge pile that I take to the Island Laundromat once a week."

A gust of wind swept through the RV site, causing my teeth to chatter. "Call me if you find anything suspicious."

"Will do." He disappeared into the darkness, and I heard the roar of a motorcycle engine that then faded into the distance.

He must've been parked on the other side of my mystery neighbor.

Standing there for a few moments, I debated whether or not to call Pop Pop and fill him in on Coop's intel. But I really didn't have much new to pass on, and the "horrible boss" thing would only fuel my undercover handyman's union-organizing frenzy.

Another gust of wind swept through, and Kong gave a loud, irritated bark.

Pop Pop would have to wait.

I unlocked the Airstream door, swung it open, and scooped up Kong in my arms. No adoring licks greeted me, just another annoyed bark. Apologizing to my pooch, I grabbed his leash and started for the beach at the moment when a woman with long, dark hair and enormous, tortoiseshell sunglasses came barreling around the back of my silver-hulled trailer.

"I've gotta get out of here. Now," she pronounced. The breeze whipped her hair forward, partially obscuring her face.

Startled, I peered at her through the dim light of my outside awning lights, taking in the heavy makeup, dangling earrings, and gold skintight pants topped by a black sequined sweatshirt. Something seemed vaguely familiar.

She pulled her hair back, dipped the sunglasses down on her nose, and pointed at her election button. "It's me. Wanda Sue."

"Why are you wearing a wig?"

"Honey, I needed a disguise 'cause I'm officially on the lam. I heard on the island grapevine that the police found out Bucky was attacked with a frying pan, so now I'm the number-one suspect. It's only a matter of time before they haul me into the slammer."

"Okay, let's just calm down and stop using words like 'lam' and 'slammer.' Where did you hear that kind of stuff anyway?"

"Classic Movie Channel."

"Things have changed since Jimmy Cagney was *The Public Enemy.*"

Kong yapped with a high-pitched bark that told me his need for walkies was beyond urgent. "Wanda Sue, you can't just leave the island if the police need to question you."

"I'm not leaving; I'm just going underground. It's a big island. I'll just disappear."

"Coral Island is only twelve miles long. Where could you go?"

"I've got my plan."

Kong yanked at his leash.

I gave him a little pat to calm him. "Look, Wanda Sue, you're overreacting. You know Nick Billie. He's not going to do anything that isn't fair and reasonable. And if he needs to talk with you as a person of interest—"

"A what?" Her eyes turned wild. "Did he say he was going to question me?"

"Um . . . maybe." I touched her arm. "But you don't have anything to worry about. You didn't kill Bucky. Nick knows that. And I've got my top-notch team at the *Observer* investigating every lead."

"That old bag, Bernice, and the kid with the cell phone?"

"Not exactly. Bernice broke her arm. But I still have Joe Earl. And don't forget Madame Geri," I added with a hopeful smile. Granted, she was a few notches down from top, but I knew Wanda Sue respected her psychic prowess.

My landlady paused, then shook her head. "Even Madame Geri can't help me now." She rammed the sunglasses back in place, transforming her appearance into a kind of Nicki Minaj-meets-midlife look. "Mallie, hon, I'll never forget what a good friend you've been to me, and that's why I'm going to turn over the Twin Palms to you. You're the new manager. Watch over the park, will ya? And don't worry, Pop Pop is taking all of his medications; I checked. So he can help you. Lordy, I'll miss you and that old man." She sniffed back a few tears. "I forwarded your cell-phone number to all of the site renters in case they have any problems. You'll be fine."

"Oh, no. That's not a happening option."

Kong yanked his leash in the direction of the nearest cabbage palm, and I looked down at him with a severe glare. By the time I tipped my head back in Wanda Sue's direction, she was gone. Vanished like a spandex and sequined ghost.

"Wanda Sue!" I shouted into the wind as I scurried around the beach to see if I could catch a glimpse of where she'd fled, but I didn't see so much as a footprint in the sand.

Jeez.

This was not happening. I was now in charge of the RV park, in addition to the *Observer.*

Could it get any worse?

Kong peed on my shoe.

CHAPTER ELEVEN

Before Kong could do any more damage to my running shoes, I hustled him over to the nearest sea oats as I ducked behind a palm tree to block the wind. Then I whipped out my cell phone. Already, I had a text message from someone in the park named "Beachybabe54" who couldn't get her cable-TV plug to work on her site.

I closed my eyes briefly for a "muggatoni mantra" to calm myself.

After a few moments of peaceful pasta images, I hit the speed-dial number for Pop Pop's cell, praying he'd pick up. I needed him back here even more urgently than I needed him undercover at the tilapia farm. Besides, he'd seemed to have been side-tracked by the plight of his fellow geriatric workers, so I wasn't sure how much real information I was going to get out of him.

"United Tilapia Farmworkers Union," he answered, and I clenched my teeth.

"Pop Pop, this is Mallie." I enunciated each word carefully, in case his hearing aid batteries were out. "I know you're undercover, but I sure could use you back here at the Twin Palms. Wanda Sue just decided to take a little . . . trip, and there's no one here to check people in or park their rigs on the sites."

"Impossible," he replied, using the Spanish pronunciation. "I think I'm on to something here. From what I've been able to glean from Pepe and Jose, that *hombre,* Travis, was dumping

bleach in the fish tanks. They think he's trying to *kill* the tilapia."

A little lurch of excitement tugged inside of me, momentarily causing me to forget the fact that a thin layer of wool stood between me and the biting offshore gusts. "Are you sure it's not chlorine?"

"I scooped out some of the water in the tanks, and did a little taste. It's bleach, all right. I can tell the difference after maintaining the Twin Palms swimming pool all these years. Chlorine will kill algae, but bleach will kill the fish."

"That might connect with something Coop told me about Travis watching him every time he was at the tilapia farm. He might've been worried that Coop would find out what was going on with the tanks." I did a little fist pump in triumph, momentarily distracted from my situation at the Twin Palms. At least, I'd guessed that part correctly.

"Why would Travis the Tyrant sabotage his own operation?" Pop Pop queried with impressive alliteration.

"I haven't figured out that part yet. It's puzzling, but significant, I'm sure." I edged around the palm tree to check on Kong, and the wind hit me with a hard blast. I ducked behind the tree again, my legs shaking and teeth chattering. *Okay, time to wrap it up.* "Do you have any bleach evidence?"

"I've got the plastic jug in my hand right now, *chica.*"

"Um . . . why are you speaking Spanish?"

"I've picked up some words from my new *amigos* while we've been writing a list of worker demands." He rustled some papers. "They need two Geritol breaks a day, an hour for lunch, and a daily siesta. And that's only the beginning. We haven't even started on benefits like discounted bifocals or long-term nursing care. *Viva la libertad!*"

"Just be careful. You don't want to get those guys in trouble and cause them to lose their jobs."

"Hah! If Travis makes any move to fire us for organizing, I'll call in the teamsters. We know our rights, even if we are all over seventy."

I gnawed on my lower lip nervously. "Don't get too riled up, and make sure you take your blood-pressure medication."

"Si."

"All right, Pop Pop, stay where you are, for now. But keep nosing around for incriminating evidence against Travis. That's the important thing. Tomorrow morning, I'll try and line up someone else to take over at the Twin Palms while Wanda Sue is gone, then I'll head over to the tilapia farm to pick up the bleach bottle from you. Hook it onto your oxygen tank, so you remember."

"Gotta go. We're having a late-night solidarity rally at Le Sink. You might want to join us."

"I'll pass, but thanks anyway."

"Okay, *chica. Adios.*" He clicked off, and I held out the cell phone, not sure whether I should be frustrated or worried. Either way, I was definitely picking him up tomorrow. At the very least he'd be fired, and at the worst, he'd be jailed for being a public nuisance.

Kong popped around the palm tree, tail wagging.

"Let's get inside. I've lost feeling in my feet." I took a quick glance out over the Gulf. While I'd been occupied with Wanda Sue's trauma, the sun had dipped below the horizon, causing deep, blood-red colors to spark across the sky in jagged streaks. A shiver snaked through me that had nothing to do with the evening chill; I'd never seen a sky that color before.

My cell phone rang again, and I reluctantly checked the number. Right now, I wasn't up for another nastygram from Liz Ellis or an RV-park resident with a clogged sewer pipe.

When I saw the caller, though, I exhaled in relief.

"Aunt Lily, I just saw the weirdest sunset. You know, the kind that looks like the sky is bleeding? It's creepy. What's that saying? 'Red sky at night'—"

" 'Sailor's delight,' " she finished ironically.

"Oh."

"It means good weather is coming. The red sky at morning is the sailor's warning of bad weather."

"I'll check it when I get up." Like I'd be up at dawn—hah.

"Weather predictions aside, I just had a strange message from Wanda Sue saying she was turning over the Twin Palms to you to manage because she was now on the run from the law and would be living the rest of her life as a fugitive."

"Did she bring up the orange coveralls?"

"I believe so." Aunt Lily cleared her throat with a loud and deliberate emphasis. "Can you tell me what the hell is going on?"

Tightening my grip on Kong's leash as I hustled toward the safe (and warm) haven of my Airstream, I launched into the last twenty-four hours, sparing my great-aunt nothing.

She fell silent for a few moments after I'd spilled the whole shebang, then spoke up. "Let me get this straight. You're investigating Bucky's murder with your editor's sister who broke her arm riding a unicycle around the office, a psychic who's talking to a violin, and a seventy-something handyman who's working undercover at a tilapia farm?"

"That pretty much sums it up." I grimaced at her succinct synopsis of my Big Fat Sucky Life. "It doesn't sound so good when you put out the facts like that, but this whole 'in charge' thing is new to me."

"I don't need to tell you that Pop Pop is a senior citizen with lung problems and high blood pressure." Her voice took on an edge.

"I know, but he's taking his meds and his stint at the tilapia farm is only short-term. Twenty-four hours at most before I bring him in. On the plus side, he's already found some possible evidence, so I said I'd pick him up in the morning, but he's kind of gone off on a . . . tangent."

"And that is?"

"He's . . . uh, trying to unionize his two geriatric co-workers." I detected her gasp but kept going. "To be honest, I was surprised, too, but it may not be such a bad idea since the other two coots aren't being paid decent wages or benefits. And they might know something that we can use to bring in Bucky's killer." When in doubt, crank up the motor mouth. "Anyway, Pop Pop mentioned something about a 'solidarity rally' tonight at the Le Sink, the dumpy restaurant that he likes so much."

"I know the place." Aunt Lily ground out every word with cutting precision. "I'm sending Sam over there right now. He'll watch over Pop Pop until he gets tired of this foolishness." She murmured a few words—presumably to Sam—and I heard him give a loud laugh. At least *he* saw the humor in this situation.

"As for Wanda Sue," she continued, speaking to me again, "did she say where she was going to hide out on the island?" I heard Sam laugh again.

"Sort of. I did point out that Coral Island is only twelve miles long, so there aren't a lot of places to hole up."

"I'm sure that was helpful. I guess we'll just have to hope she doesn't do something stupid like try to hop a boat to South America. In the meantime, I'll come over and work the check-in desk at the Twin Palms. When she comes back to her senses, she won't want a big mess at the RV park."

"Perfect. I can meet you at the main office around 10ish, and we'll go over the current resident list and upcoming reservations. It's off-season, so Wanda Sue wasn't expecting too many newcomers." At least, I didn't think so. But I had no idea as to who was checking in or when. Then again, I might get a line on who had checked in next door to me. That was something at least.

"What about the park maintenance till Pop Pop returns?" she inquired. "Not that I expect him to be out long."

"Well . . . that's a tough one. There's no male under seventy at the park right now who has handyman potential."

"Except me," Cole said as he approached.

"Aunt Lily, I may have someone. See you tomorrow." I lowered the cell phone. Cole's sun-bleached hair blew in the hard breeze, soft pale strands whipping across his face. I reached out and drew the stray hair back from his forehead, a question in my eyes. "How about it? Would you mind filling in for Pop Pop for a day or two?"

"Sure."

"I can't tell you how much I appreciate it."

"It's okay. What are fiancés for?" He held my gaze steadily, a question in his eyes. "That is, if we're still engaged."

"Of course we're still engaged." The words sounded strained and hollow, as if they could barely be spoken through the filter of my own uncertainty. Okay, I'd been thinking about our relationship for a long time, mulling over every aspect of the future together. And, in my heart of hearts, I knew it wasn't a happening option.

"But you're not wearing the ring?"

"No."

How could I tell him that I'd lost it? How could I say that we'd had our shot at coupledom years ago, but it didn't pan out? How could I say that I still loved him—as a friend?

He smiled with a sad, sweet lopsided twist to his mouth as our conversation trailed off into silence; we both knew the truth.

"Keep the diamond—as a token."

"Cole, I'm sorry."

"Don't be." He took my hand and kissed it. "We'll always have Orlando."

I laughed, but felt the sting of unshed tears in my eyes.

"So what do you need me to do to help out at the RV park?" He gave my fingers a parting squeeze and let go.

"Let me think . . ." Pausing to clear my mind of the last few emotional moments, I took in a deep breath of chilly air and exhaled with a visible puff. "I've got a couple of text messages from different residents and visitors. One recent complaint about a faulty cable-TV plug, and an older one about loud music. Oh, never mind. That was from me about my possibly-famous mystery neighbor."

"I'm on it." He glanced at the large RV next door, the awning decorated with chili-pepper lights that blinked to the beat of the music. "I'll start with the cable plug and get to your complaint in the morning. That place scares me."

"Just wait till the stuffed flamingo starts playing the guitar again."

"Seriously?"

I nodded, and supplied him with the site number for the cable-plug debacle.

"By the way, where's Pop Pop?"

"Can't say. It's undercover work for the newspaper."

"And Wanda Sue?"

"She left suddenly because she was afraid of being arrested for Bucky McGuire's murder. She intends to stay on the run till the *real* killer is arrested."

"You realize how crazy your life is?" he pointed out quite unnecessarily.

"Yeah."

"You know, having someone to ground you wouldn't be a bad thing." He pressed his lips to mine, but it felt like a good-bye kiss—bittersweet. "Too bad you don't want it to be me. We had a good thing going."

Cole drew back, keeping a light hold on my shoulders for a few moments. Then he left without another word.

I stood there for a few moments, the cold forgotten as I watched him disappear into the growing darkness.

All of a sudden, I felt very alone.

"Did I just do the right thing?" I asked Kong with a sigh of frustration. "What do you think? Tap your tail once for yes, and twice for no."

He thumped his tail three times.

"You're no help."

I led my teacup poodle into the Airstream and shut the door tightly against the rest of the world. I couldn't take any more today. It was time to make dinner (frozen entrée) and have some quiet time (more *Friends* reruns).

As I hung up Kong's leash next to the door, I turned around and started. Bernice was seated on my sofa, wearing jeans and a sweatshirt, her arm in a cast, and reading one of my graphic novels: *Batgirl: Fists of Fury.*

"What are you doing here and, even more importantly, how did you get into my Airstream?"

"Get real, Miss Priss. Everybody knows you hide the key in the geranium pot outside."

"Obviously. But that doesn't mean you can use it and just let yourself in."

"The doctor said I shouldn't be alone 'cause he gave me a butt load of painkillers. With my dumb-ass sister still out of town, I had to commandeer Madame Geri to pick me up and bring me here. I couldn't stay with her because of that beady-eyed bird of hers. I'd be afraid he'd peck out my eyes in my sleep. So, it looks like it's you and me, kiddo. And this stack of comic books." She pointed at my entire *Batgirl* series on the floor next to the sofa.

"Graphic novels. And they are a legit literary genre today. And for your information, my set of Shakespeare plays and Jane Austen novels are in storage since the Airstream doesn't exactly have library-sized storage." My English-major ire stirred, I wondered if there were enough leftover pills in the "butt load" to knock her out for the night.

"Yeah, yeah." She waved off my protestations. "I'm starving. What do you have to eat?"

Kong whimpered, and I wanted to do the same.

What could I do, though?

Two hours later, I'd made Bernice dinner (another frozen entrée in the microwave), poured (and drank) a glass of cheap Flip Flop Chardonnay, watched a *CSI-Miami* rerun with her (she liked her TV grisly and gritty, not light and witty like my *Friends* addiction), and settled her on my fold-out sofa. Exhausted, I slumped into a chair with a second glass of wine.

Bernice propped herself up with a pile of pillows and sat back with her cast-encased arm cradled in front of her. "Too bad I'm taking the painkillers, or I could have a glass of wine, even if it is that cheap stuff."

I glared at her as I held up my glass that had been refilled to the brim. "And if your sister weren't such a stingy boss, I might be able to afford something better. As it stands, the Flip Flop will have to suffice." I eyed the light-gold color of the *el cheapo vino.* "It's not half bad."

"It's crap."

True.

"You know, Bernice, I can turn you out in the cold without a blink."

"Pffft," she scoffed. "Like you'd do that."

She knew me too well. "At the very least, you could try to be a little nicer since you are in my home, and I've been waiting on you hand and foot all night."

Bernice leaned her head back with a sigh, and her face seemed to sag with fatigue. Without the aging hipster outfit, overdone makeup, and fake hair, she looked like a tired and not-so-young woman who'd had a rough day. "It's not easy being me."

"Tell me something I don't know."

"No, I mean it." Her voice took on a serious tone. "It's no fun being middle-aged without a partner. You're either a chick or an old hen in our society, and my chick years are long over." She sighed again. "It was fun dating around when I was young, but now I'd like something a little more permanent. Facing old age alone is . . . scary."

My heart tugged in sympathy. "I'm sure you'll meet someone. Look at Anita and her late-life marriage to Mr. Benton." Who would've thought Bernice had a soft and vulnerable side?

She grimaced. "I'm aiming a little higher than that skinflint Benton, or that surfer-wastrel Cole you're engaged to. I'm looking for a sugar-daddy, and I intend to find one if I have to scout out every assisted-living center in Southwest Florida."

So much for the touchy-feely moment. "We're not engaged any longer."

Sinking back into her pillows, she flashed a knowing glance in my direction. "You'd better get cracking to find a replacement, kiddo, before the hen stage takes hold. Trust me." She pulled up the covers. "Now I'd like a cup of tea before I go to sleep. Chamomile with a little honey and fresh-squeezed lemon."

I rose to my feet, finishing off my wine. "You'll get a Lipton bag in tap water."

"That's something, I guess."

After making my unwanted guest a cup of tea, I retreated to my room at the back of the Airstream and collapsed on the bed, still dressed, embracing the comfort of my classic-cars sheets and pillowcase.

Kong hopped up next to me and hunkered down in the crook of my arm. I stroked his soft, curly coat and savored the blessed solitude, ready to doze off—until the loud wheeze of Bernice's snoring penetrated the stillness. A grating noise that sounded like a buzz saw cutting through wood. Groaning, I snatched up the pillow and rammed it over my face, but it didn't make a dent in muffling the snorting, lip-smacking sounds emanating from my guest.

Sitting up again, I drummed my fingers, smoothed out the sheets, and tried to meditate with my "muggatoni mantra." But nothing helped to distract me from Bernice the Buzz Saw. Fat chance that I'd get forty winks tonight—or even ten.

I changed into my PJs and hopped back into bed, hoping she'd quiet down. No such luck. If anything, the snoring grew louder. And louder.

Might as well get to work on my suspect list.

Propping up my pillow (and pounding it a few times for good measure), I leaned back and stared at the ceiling, letting my mind wander over the events of the last two days. I had three main suspects for Bucky's death: Travis, Destiny, and Liz. They were the people most closely connected with Bucky right before he was killed, with Liz as the one most likely to do bodily harm to someone suspect.

Time to tier the mental list.

Tier One: Liz Ellis—the landscaping client from hell with a hair-trigger temper. Her razor-sharp vitriol on Bucky's blog seemed one step away from a physical shiv. Not to mention, she seemed to toss around lawsuit threats with the casual flick of a legal flyswatter.

Tier Two: Travis—the ex-partner who held a major grudge against Bucky for supposedly embezzling money from their company, and who may or may not be guilty of fish murder. He, too, possessed a hair-trigger temper.

Tier Three: Destiny—the woman who loved him and seemed destroyed by Bucky's death. Or was she? Her over-the-top emotional display *seemed* real enough, but she appeared to be jealous and possessive. And (what a surprise!) she showed every sign of (guess what?) a hair-trigger temper.

One thing I knew for certain: All three needed anger management, and *I* didn't want to be on the receiving end of any of their rageaholic displays.

What about Wanda Sue? For certain, she didn't murder Bucky.

She might've threatened him with a frying pan when their relationship was heading for the skids, but she never would have actually struck him with it. She did *not* have a hair-trigger temper—not that I'd ever seen. Granted, she had engaged in a verbal fracas with Destiny and threatened to "take it outside," and, yes, she did fire a flare gun at the town-hall meeting. All true. But she said she'd aimed that gun away from Bucky toward the ceiling, and I believed her—sort of. I swallowed hard.

Better stop right there. The facts weren't exactly tallying up on Wanda Sue's side, and I was running out of time and tiers on my list.

Tomorrow I had to get it in gear, and not just for the murder case. I had to finish the *Observer* final copy edits for the printer, get the Twin Palms RV Park problem solved, and, most importantly, make certain Pop Pop didn't turn into a card-carrying, union-loving socialist or get himself killed.

Bernice's snoring amped up into a deep-throated, window-shaking cacophony.

This day would never end.

I rummaged around in my built-in dresser drawers and found a pair of swimmers' earplugs that I'd bought when I thought I was going to hit the waves for exercise. (I'd never opened the packet.)

Ripping open the plastic cover, I then jammed them in, and threw the covers over my face.

Kong ducked under with me, tucking his paws around his head.

Bleary-eyed and groggy the next morning, I rolled out of bed and glared at Bernice on my way to the coffee pot. How is it one human being could make so many grotesque (and earplug piercing) noises when sleeping? Between her snoring, wheezing, and coughing, I barely managed to get four hours of sleep.

"Get up on the wrong side of the bed, Miss Priss?" she asked in a chipper voice, stretched out on my sofa, fully dressed with the wig in place. "Not me. I slept like a log. Must've been the painkillers they gave me at the hospital. Whew. That stuff really knocks you out. But I'm up and ready for action now. Just to show you how much I appreciate your dingy trailer hospitality, I'm gonna help Madame Geri with that stupid violin story once we get to the office."

"Should you be working with your injury and that cast?" I pulled my Jumped-up Java full-bodied roast out of the cabinet and shoveled three heaping scoops into the filter of my Mr. Coffee.

Bernice thumped her cast. "Get real. I'm indestructible."

"Yeah. You're like a tank."

"You betcha, Miss Priss." She adjusted the wig. "I just need you to make my lunch, drive me to work, and set me up at your computer. Otherwise, I can handle the rest. Just call me Superwoman."

Rolling my eyes, I figured there was no point in asking her to tail Destiny with her invalid needs right now.

"But first. I can't get this cast wet, so I'll need some help with washing my face and putting on my makeup. I could manage the wig, but that's a one-arm task."

I froze, coffee pot in hand.

Was I to be spared nothing?

An hour later, after fortifying myself with high-test caffeine, I oversaw some awkward face-washing procedures and makeup applications. It wasn't pretty. But, eventually, I finished up with minimal trauma, and we were both seated in my truck, wearing our jeans and sweatshirts and heading to the Twin Palms main office. Aunt Lily was already pacing outside, wearing a green sweater, tailored pants, and a stern-faced expression. She held up her arm and tapped her silver Brighton watch.

I grimaced. This was going to take some finessing. "Bernice, after all the morning exertions, why don't you stay in the truck?"

She glanced at my great-aunt's pinched mouth and clutched her cast in a protective clasp. "Good idea."

As I slid out of Rusty and made my way over to Aunt Lily, I launched into a motor mouth extravaganza. "I know I'm half an hour late, but Bernice showed up last night with her broken arm in a cast. She couldn't be alone. So she slept on my sofa and kept me up with her snoring all night. Not to mention I had to help her get ready this morning. Sorry."

Aunt Lily glanced at Bernice, who was drawing an obscene hand gesture on her own cast with a magic marker, then back at me. "I guess you've been punished enough this morning."

"It was pure torture." I dug into my hobo bag and pulled out Wanda Sue's set of keys. "Can you let yourself into the main office? This Bernice thing has set me behind, and I've only got an hour to get this week's *Observer* copy to the printer. Then I've got to meet Pop Pop."

"You'd better tell me that you're picking him up and bringing him back here." Her arched brows moved up a fraction. "I don't need to mention that he can't take too much more of this craziness at his age."

"I promise." I held out the keys and gave them a little jingle. "All you have to do is stand guard at the desk in case anyone checks in today. Wanda Sue keeps the guest ledger and welcome packets in the file cabinet. Nothing is computerized, so it's pretty simple. I'll be back by lunchtime with Pop Pop in tow. And, in the meantime, Cole said he'd take care of any maintenance issues that come up. Okay?"

Shaking her head, Lily stretched out her hand, and I dropped the keys into her palm. "All right but, after this, we're going to sit down and have a long, serious talk about the way you're living your life. Do you know that Sam practically had to drag Pop Pop and his work friends out of Le Sink last night because they were doing tequila shots? A man his age? They all spent the night at Sam's house and then took off this morning to meet some union big shot at the tilapia farm. I shudder to think what will happen if this whole union thing goes through. Apparently, Pop Pop was boasting last night about spreading the word to every business on the island."

I opened my mouth to defend myself, but Aunt Lily averted her head. "I don't want to hear it."

"But—" My cell phone jingled, and I glanced at the number. *Speak of the devil.*

"If that's Pop Pop, you'd better tell him to stop this foolishness before he ends up in the hospital. Whatever happens to him is on your head, Mallie." She turned on her heel and stomped toward the office entrance.

I flipped open the phone. "Pop Pop, maybe you need to back off."

"What? Not when I'm on to something."

I waited a few seconds until Aunt Lily had disappeared inside. Then I strolled toward my truck just to provide extra distance between her sharp hearing and me. "Okay, what's the scoop? Did you catch Travis dumping the bleach in the fish tanks?"

"Nope. Even better."

"Poison?"

"Hah!" He gave a snort of triumph. "We've got a union

organizer from Tallahassee coming down here this morning."

My heart sank.

"This guy is going to help us hold an election. Before the day is out, we'll be the official United Tilapia Farm Workers. That'll show Mr. Big Shot Travis."

I snapped the phone shut and hopped back into my truck, slamming the door so hard, the entire vehicle shook with the force. "Don't say a word." I enunciated each word as I pointed a finger at Bernice, then jammed on my seat belt.

"Hey, don't take it out on me that your old fossil of an ex-boyfriend can't do simple surveillance work."

"He's not my ex-boyfriend! I'm engaged to Cole. At least, I was until last night. And I don't know if I made the right decision or not." I cranked Rusty into reverse. "This whole multi-tasking/management thing is stressing me out beyond belief."

"Jeez, stop whining. *I'm* the one with a broken arm, which, by the way, is hurting like hell in spite of the cool doodles and signatures on my cast." She gestured at the outline of a fist—middle finger extended up—and large, sloppy writing that spelled out "Arm Candy Hottie."

"You wrote that hottie comment yourself."

She shrugged. "The truth is the truth."

"Oh, take a pain pill." I shifted into forward and revved off.

"Hey, Miss Priss, I'm sorry about your man trouble, but it's your own fault." Bernice pulled out her painkillers, shook the bottle, and popped one. "Just make a decision about your love life and stick with it. And don't be a wuss about it. If you don't want to marry Cole, then don't. If you want my take on it, he seemed a little too veggie omelet to me anyway. You're a fast-food kind of gal."

I couldn't help nodding in agreement.

"What you really need is a lifestyle coach and mentor. Like yours truly. I decided to change my look and start trolling for a man when my lame-ass sister landed herself a man. If it wasn't too late for a hag bag like Anita, I realized the guys would be lining up for me. You're never too old to imitate Lady Gaga. You should try it sometime. It might help you attract a better quality type of guy."

"Thanks for the advice," I commented drily. "But I think I'll stick with my own judgment on my love life."

"Suit yourself. We both see how successful that's been."

We drove in silence for a few minutes along Cypress Drive, with only a few other cars on the road this early.

As we passed a mango grove, I thought I heard an odd rattling sound waft through the truck. "Bernice, are you shaking that pill bottle?"

"What are you talking about? I put it back in my purse."

The loud staccato noise continued, almost like the shaking of a baby rattle, followed by a soft, slithering sound.

My breath caught in my throat.

Snake?

A cold chill washed over me that had nothing to do with the morning air. Chewing on my lower lip, I glanced nervously in the rearview mirror and scanned the backseat . . . then bit my tongue in panic.

A rattlesnake with black-edged brown diamonds patterned on his back lay coiled on the seat, staring right at me and shaking his tail—ready to strike.

Uh-oh.

CHAPTER TWELVE

"Don't move," I whispered to Bernice, keeping my upper body as motionless as possible, while fighting the urge to ram down the brake.

"Speak up, Miss Priss." She cupped her ear and leaned in my direction. The movement caused Mr. Snake to twist his head toward Bernice, his forked tongue darting in and out.

Flashing a warning glance at her, I eased my foot up on the gas. "Shut up and stay still while I bring Rusty to a stop," I said out of the side of my mouth in a low, even tone. "That rattle we've been hearing is a diamondback rattlesnake on the backseat. Don't turn around, for God's sake." I took another brief peep in the rearview mirror. "He looks ready to strike."

Bernice froze, her hand remaining at her ear. "Are you sure it's a rattlesnake?" she murmured.

"Oh, yeah." I noted the snake's tail with its brown stripes ending in a button-like nub that flicked back and forth like a whip.

The rattling sound grew louder.

Sweat broke out on the back of my neck at the realization that one quick strike of the snake could be the end for me. I was going to die. I knew it. And, even worse, the last person I'd see alive was Bernice.

My truck gradually slowed to a stop, right in the middle of Cypress Road. Keeping my foot on the brake, I didn't dare turn the wheel to steer off to the side onto the gravel; any big, sudden movement could cause the snake to attack. Luckily, there wasn't any traffic—yet.

We both sat there, engine idling, not speaking or moving. Finally, Bernice spoke up in a hoarse whisper, "What's the plan? I've got an itch under my cast."

"I . . . I don't know." Once again, my eyes shifted to the rearview mirror. Mr. Snake remained in the same position, but had reverted to staring at me alone through his narrow lizard eyes. Eek. My heart was thumping so hard in my chest that I was sure Mr. Snake could sense it. "Once he goes to sleep, we can ease open the doors and get out. We just need to stay calm and not move too quickly."

"How are we going to know he's asleep?"

"I guess when he puts his head down."

Just then, I heard a loud honking horn and shifted my glance to the road behind us: a monster truck with a pickup body and large wheels was bearing down at high speed, aimed right at us. Another honk alerted me and my glance shifted forward to spy a compact car speeding toward us.

"Bernice, do you see what I see?"

"Sure do. If the snake doesn't kill us, the truck-car sandwich will."

"Is your door unlocked?"

A few seconds passed. "Yes."

"Okay." I took in a deep breath. "On my mark, we're going to have to throw open the doors. Then, jump and roll. I can't chance hitting the gas pedal."

"What about Rusty?"

I gave the wheel a miniscule pat. "He would understand. It's us or the snake."

The truck's horn came in a loud, long blast, causing the snake to jerk his head away from us.

"Now! Do it!"

Simultaneously, we jerked on our door handles, lurched out of the truck and rolled away from my vehicle. I hit hard against the cold asphalt, then spun over and over, praying that neither of the vehicles would flatten me into roadkill. I heard Bernice scream and curse with a new string of profanities like I'd never heard before, even from her. She must've hit the road hard with her cast.

I rolled onto the loose pebbles and dirt just at the moment the compact car that had been coming at us whizzed past with a blast of wind. But I kept rolling and didn't stop until I slammed into a thick palm tree trunk.

Raising my head, I caught a glimpse of the black and gold monster truck as it swerved around Rusty. The driver didn't even spare us a glance. I leapt to my feet, adrenaline pumping, and shook my fist at him, adding a few choice curses of my own.

"I broke my damn cast! Hell and damnation!" Bernice exclaimed from the other side of the road. She lay on her back and, after a couple of failed attempts, hoisted herself up into a sitting position. She held up her arm, pointing at the cast, which was cracked in two, connected only by a plaster thread.

"Are you okay?" I steadied myself against the palm tree, trying to catch my breath. Remarkably, Rusty remained idling on the road.

"No, I'm not! Dammit, I think I broke my wrist on the other arm now!"

"Impossible."

"Au contraire." Bernice held up the opposite arm, and I could see that her hand hung at a crooked angle.

The compact car had halted a little farther down the road, and a young, female driver sprang out, sprinting towards us, her cell phone in hand. "I'm sorry that I didn't stop, but I could see that maniac in the truck wasn't slowing down. In fact, I think he went faster. I thought he was going to hit you."

"Me, too." My breathing still ragged, I brushed off my jeans with a shaky hand, noting that I had a couple of scratches on my forearm from the gravel.

"Do you want me to call 9-1-1?" she asked, pushing back her long, brown hair with a shaky hand.

"Bernice? Do you need an ambulance?" I queried in a loud voice.

"No. Just a ride to the ER, you dummy."

Momentarily tempted to leave Bernice on the side of the road, I gave myself a three-second fantasy of driving off alone, and then handed the young woman my card. "Could you write down your name and number? I want to report this incident to the island police."

"Sure thing." She complied and handed back my card. "I even snapped a picture of the truck with my phone."

"Can you pull it up?"

She tapped on the camera icon, then frowned in exasperation. "I can't make out the license plate." She held it up, and I squinted to make out anything but a blurry truck bumper.

Damn.

"Sorry."

We tried enlarging the photo, but that only made the license plate even more grainy.

"Hel-lo? Could we hold off on the selfies?" Bernice called out. "I'm in pain over here."

After having her message me the picture, I waved off our Good Samaritan. "Did you see the snake slip out of Rusty?" I asked Bernice, tiptoeing across Cypress Road, watchful for traffic. And the rattler.

She nodded. "He slithered into the saw palmetto stand right after the monster truck went by." Bernice tried to flex her wrist and winced in pain. "Did you recognize that jerkface in the truck?"

"Nope. The driver had on a baseball cap, so I couldn't tell if it was a man or a woman. It might've looked from behind like we were just casually stopped in the middle of the road, but the driver should've at least slowed down." I helped Bernice to her feet and, as I guided her back towards Rusty, I added, "That young woman who stopped said it looked like the truck actually sped up, like he was aiming for us . . ." my voice trailed off as I peered through the window into the back seat from a discreet distance, just to make certain Bernice was right about the reptile's exit.

No snake.

Whew.

I took in a deep, calming breath. "All clear."

"Told you."

"There's nothing wrong with a double check. I don't want to see another snake that close up, ever." After settling Bernice into the passenger seat, I took my place behind the wheel and texted Joe Earl to let him know what had happened.

"What did you mean just now?" She cradled both the broken arm and possibly broken wrist.

"First, we find a rattlesnake in the backseat, but my windows were closed, so someone must've put it there last night. Then, a truck comes barreling down the road, almost like it was targeting us where we were stopped." I eased Rusty forward, my hands clenching the wheel. "Doesn't that seem like an unusual coincidence?"

"Now that you mention it, yeah." She winced in pain again. "Let's talk about your half-baked theories, Miss Priss, *after* we go to the hospital."

"Hey, if you want a ride to the ER, try being a little nicer to me. I'm all you've got right now with Anita still out of town."

"Oh, bite me." She leaned back against the seat and closed her eyes.

"Bad word choice, after the snake incident."

"Fine. Bug off."

I wondered if I could break her leg to go along with the other injured appendages as I stepped on the gas.

An hour later, I rushed into the *Observer* office and made a beeline for Anita's office, not looking right or left.

After spending an interminable hour getting Bernice checked into the ER, I had to leave her there, knowing I had precious little time to get back to the newspaper to e-mail the final copy edits to the printer. Talk about a tight deadline.

"How's Bernice?" Joe Earl inquired as I streaked past him.

"Fine." I didn't break my pace but, out of the corner of my eye, I caught sight of him seated at my desk with Madame Geri hovering nearby. "Can't talk now. I've got to—"

"Get the edition out?" A familiar voice stopped me in my tracks. Was it possible? Smiling, I turned to see Sandy, at her desk.

I gave her a quick hug, noting her glowing face and happy grin. "Obviously, marriage agrees with you."

"You could say that. Our honeymoon in St. Augustine was just magical, and Jimmy is the best husband ever." Her smile upped to a megawatt beam of happiness. "Life is good."

I grinned back, but it felt halfhearted after the events of the last twenty-four hours. My own engagement had officially tanked, and I didn't even have the ring as a memento. Not to mention, I'd had a near-death experience this morning before my first Krispy Kreme or second round of coffee. "Can't talk now. I've got to finish up those copy edits."

"Already done," Sandy sang out. "When Joe Earl told me that you'd probably be late, I pulled it up on Anita's computer and proofread the mockup. All you need to do is add the headline and send it off. The repair guy also showed up this morning." She gestured toward the new, gleaming glass around my boss's cubicle. No tape. No cardboard. "By the way, we added Madame Geri's violin story to the lower half of the front page, stressing its *history.*"

Joe Earl gave a thumbs-up; Madame Geri gave a thumbs-down.

"You're the best, Sandy." I could already feel the pressure easing.

"One last item: I found this in the lower file drawer of your desk; it was in a folder." She held up my engagement ring, the stones glinting with a pure, white light.

"OMG." My mouth dropped open. "I'd put in the top drawer, and it must've fallen down. I didn't think to look there. Duh." I clasped the ring tightly in my palm. I had a memento of my time with Cole after all.

A tiny glow lit inside of me.

"If you'd asked me, I could've found it. Or at least posed a question to the Abe Lincoln violin. Speaking of which, I'm done with journalism." Madame Geri cleared her throat and threw the *Dummy's Guide* in the trash can. "I'm not pleased that my article is below the fold, and neither is Old Abe."

"My apologies to you and the president, but I think I'll go with Sandy's office skills over your quasi-intuitive mumbo jumbo." I couldn't hide the triumph—or sarcasm—in my voice. "Where's Marley?"

"Home, I think," Madame Geri said. "I'm not sure, since I lost his pet pager."

"Maybe you should ask the violin his whereabouts," I couldn't resist adding, happy as a lark that the beady-eyed parrot wasn't in the office. She glared at me.

Refusing to let her rain on my almost-have-the-edition-out

parade, I strolled into Anita's office, took her seat, and added a headline to the *Observer* front page: "Town-Council Candidate Found Dead." Sitting there with my index finger poised over the "enter" key for a few seconds, self-satisfaction flooded through my being.

I hit the button.

Now I'm an editor.

Savoring the moment, I sat back in Anita's chair, my hands folded behind my head. *I did it.* The only thing left to do was find a way to prove Wanda Sue's innocence and bring her home. *Rock on.*

A tap on the newly-installed glass window broke into my elated reverie.

"Can I talk with you?" Coop mouthed the words against the glass. I motioned him in.

Weaving around the messy stacks of old newspapers and general clutter, he took a seat across from me. "I found something that triggered a memory about Bucky."

"Do tell." Eagerly I propped my elbows on the desk, leaning forward.

"I went through all of my shirts and couldn't find anything of interest. But then I checked all of my work jeans' pockets, and saw this." He produced a small yellow Post-it note and set it on the desk.

Quickly I scanned it.

Take fertilizer to Liz Ellis's nursery.

I looked up, puzzled.

"Turn it over."

On the other side of the Post-it, the words *bad stuff* had been scrawled.

Coop tapped the note with his finger. "Bucky had me using this new fertilizer on Liz Ellis's nursery and, after a couple of weeks, I noticed it seemed to be killing the plants."

"You're the plant killer!" I exclaimed before I could stop myself.

"No!" He held up both palms in protest. "I swear I told Bucky that something was wrong with that fertilizer. I wrote the note to myself to remember to tell him that it was bad stuff. It's the truth."

"I believe you." Patting his hand, I tried to reassure him. "Sorry, that just slipped out. You're no plant killer. I know that."

He slumped back into the chair with an audible exhale of relief.

"When did you tell Bucky?"

"I don't remember that part." Coop sighed.

"Or what he did about it?"

He shook his head. "It's frustrating not having a good memory."

"I can only imagine." Looking at the Post-it again, I tried to figure out how the note might tie into Bucky's death, but I was having a hard time focusing after my near-death experiences this morning.

"Wish I could help more," Coop said.

"You did a lot. Thanks." Pushing myself to a standing position, I moved toward the doorway and stuck my head out. "Joe Earl, do you still have Liz Ellis's address? I want to talk with her."

"Sure do." He rose, snatching up his iPhone. "But I'm going with you, especially after that run-in with her outside the Shoreline Bank. She's a nasty piece of work."

"Agreed, on both counts." Liz's obnoxious personality aside, after that snake thing, I didn't particularly want to be driving alone. Whoever killed Bucky might have me next on his (or her) list.

"You know Liz Ellis?" Sandy piped up.

"Unfortunately, yes."

"She's a b-atch." Sandy's glow dimmed as her mouth took on an unpleasant twist. "When Bernice was in charge, Liz wanted to buy advertising for her nursery and . . . well, let's just say, after talking with Liz on the phone, Bernice wouldn't give her so much as a one-line ad."

"Up front and in person is even worse," I quipped. Then I jotted down Pop Pop's cell-phone number, still worried that he might be getting himself into trouble with that union organizing. "Sandy, would you call Pop Pop and just check in? He's . . . uh . . . getting some info at Tropical Tilapia, and I want to make sure he's okay. And check that he's taking his medication, too."

"No problemo." She grabbed the number from me and picked up the phone.

"Watch that Ellis woman," Coop warned. "She threw a rake at me once when I did something wrong at her nursery."

"You remembered that?"

He held up another Post-it that said, *Liz Ellis attacked me with a rake.* "I found this one in the same pocket."

Yikes.

"I agree. Be careful." Madame Geri warned as I trooped past her and motioned for Joe Earl to follow. "The spirit world told me she had a bad aura with all shades of brown. Not good."

A twinge of caution tugged at me, but I tried to shrug it off as just the ravings of a pseudo-psychic. Still . . . Madame Geri managed to be right more times than not. "Maybe you ought to keep your cell phone handy, just to play it safe. We'll call if there's a problem." We exited the office, and I noticed the sky had clouded up after a clear morning.

"Did you get a financial statement on Travis's company?" I queried as we headed toward my truck.

"Just this morning. The annual report that went out to his shareholders looked strong. Everything in the black. He was even adding assets by buying island businesses that had gone bankrupt."

"Really? That wouldn't jibe with my theory of why he might be killing his tilapia." Another dead end.

"That surprised me, too. But the spreadsheets don't lie."

"You can read an Excel spreadsheet?" I couldn't balance my checkbook.

"High-school accounting. It really came in handy when I was running my eBay sales."

"So, we're back to the question of why Travis would sabotage a thriving business," I said, half to myself. We were close. I could feel it.

"Dunno." Joe Earl gave me Liz's address, and I drove toward Paradisio, the small fishing village that separated Coral Island from the mainland. Rows of tiny, vividly colored dwellings lined the main road, some renovated with a fresh coat of paint and some unchanged from the fifties with sagging exteriors and ramshackle porches. A mixed bag of old and new.

"Could Travis have cooked the books?"

"Unlikely. The info they post online is reviewed by state auditors."

"You learned that, too, in the accounting class?"

"Yep." He glanced down at his iPhone, then pointed at a large tree with purple flowers. "MapQuest says take the next left, right there next to the royal palm tree."

As I glanced at the sagging, brown palm fronds, a sudden thought occurred to me. "Maybe the deadly fertilizer is what made Liz post those vicious comments about Bucky on his blog."

"She sure did a number on him."

"Didn't she call him a crudball?"

"Cretin."

"Let's see if we can get her to explain why she made the

posts. You never know. With her temper, she might let something slip." I made the turn at the "dead end" sign on Baypoint and steered Rusty down a narrow street where the houses grew larger and more ornate the closer we came to Paradisio Bay.

Everyone with money wanted a place on the "big water," and it appeared that all the smallish homes at the end of road had long been torn down. In their place stood faux-Mediterranean monstrosities with Spanish-tile roofs and huge sweeping verandas across the front.

Joe Earl pointed at a luxury residence complete with two-storied, arched entrance, lots of windows, and even a turret on the north side. I spied a canopy tent in the back.

"Looks like the nursery is behind the house." I took in the sickly bougainvillea bushes and withering magnolia trees that lined either side of the driveway. "Things certainly look a little droopy."

"Go figure."

I parked, and we moved toward the tall, double front doors, each with etched, oval glass. After I rang the doorbell, I took a quick backward glance at Rusty. He certainly looked more at home in an RV park than a ritzy neighborhood. "Maybe my truck needs a new coat of paint."

Before Joe Earl could respond, the door swung open, and Liz Ellis appeared, wearing a skintight, flame-orange sheath and a scowl. Her face wasn't blotchy from crying anymore, but the red rings around her eyes suggested she had still shed a few more tears over Bucky.

"What the hell do you nitwits want?" she demanded.

Charming.

"Hi, Liz. You remember us? Mallie and Joe Earl from the *Observer*?"

"Yeah."

"If you remember, you originally came by the office a couple of days ago about your dying plants and threatened me if I didn't do something about it. And I believe you followed up with several e-mails?" I gave her my best smile.

Her scowl deepened. "And I threatened you with a lawsuit for harassing me about Bucky."

"Let's just put that aside for now and focus on your nursery."

"It's just about done for now. Too little, too late," she spat out. "And I had to take a quick, high-interest loan on the house to pump some money into it, so I'll probably lose that, too."

"I'm so sorry. But I do have some information that might be pertinent to saving what's left of your plants."

"Forget it. I don't care anymore." She tried to yank the door closed again, but Joe Earl had caught the handle. She jerked it one more time, but he held fast with a tight grip that bespoke hours and hours of clutching his iPhone. "Okay, suit yourself." She stepped back with a shrug.

We followed her into a huge, high-ceilinged great room decorated with massive, antique furniture, the sofas and chairs upholstered in thick leopard and zebra skins. It looked like Jungle Larry's version of the *Antique Roadshow,* a flash and trash safari of bad taste. As Liz strolled toward the bar, Joe Earl elbowed me in the direction of a tiger-skin rug, head intact, mouth opened, and teeth bared.

I gasped and edged around it.

As we seated ourselves on one of the animal-skin sofas, Liz joined us, a half-empty iced tea–sized glass in hand. I got a whiff of gin.

She collapsed into a chair and let her head flop back, her glass tipping ice cubes onto her dress. She didn't notice. "So what's this 'pertinent' BS all about?"

Pulling out my notepad, I flipped a few pages and pretended to read aloud. "While I was researching your complaint, I found out that Bucky was using a poisonous fertilizer on your plants."

"What?" Her head snapped up. "He was deliberately destroying my nursery?"

"We don't know that," Joe Earl cut in. "One of his employees told us about the fertilizer, but he didn't remember when he'd told Bucky."

"It was that moron, Coop!" she snarled, her face bunching up with anger. "He did it. Bucky would never do something like that to me."

"Why would Coop tell us about the fertilizer if he was the one using it to kill your plants?" I pointed out, trying to gauge how much of her reaction was fueled by the alcohol or if she was using it as a smokescreen to hide something.

"All I know is it wasn't Bucky." She took another deep swig of her drink.

"So, you had no idea that he might've been the plant killer you told me about?" I pressed.

"Of course not." She began to slur her words as her glance darted back and forth between Joe Earl and me. "What are you getting at?"

"Whoever killed Bucky must've been pretty angry with him," I speculated.

"Exactly! He was murdered by that tramp, Wanda Sue," she exclaimed. "I heard the police found her frying pan, and everybody on the island knows it. If I get my hands on her, I'll make sure she regrets what she did to my sweet Bucky."

"Ms. Ellis, I'd like to remind you that Wanda Sue has not been convicted of anything."

"She did it! Everybody knows she tried to kill him with that pan years ago because she never got over his leaving her. He'd moved on to someone better." She raised her glass and stared at the contents.

I cleared my throat. "Do you mean yourself? Were you involved with Bucky when he was dating Wanda Sue?"

"You bet your sweet bippie I was." Her eyes began to tear up. "He loved me, but Wanda Sue wouldn't let him go. It was horrible. He told me that she called him constantly and threatened him. Eventually, he broke it off with her because he was worried that Wanda Sue might harm *me.*" She thumped the glass against her chest for emphasis, then began sobbing.

I took a nervous glance at Joe Earl. He looked as if he'd eaten something sour, and he clutched his iPhone so tightly, his knuckles had turned white.

Maybe it was time to wind up the interview.

"You should know that Wanda Sue had been out of the picture for some time," I said, shutting my notepad.

"I know he was engaged to someone else, that S.O.B!" Liz's chest pounding halted as her eyes narrowed into slits. She hurled her glass across the room. It hit the stone fireplace and shattered into a gazillion pieces. "He wouldn't tell me who it was, but I'm going to make it my business to find his latest girlfriend."

Cray cray.

"Speaking of business." I found my voice after a quick check of my jeans for glass fragments. "In spite of what you just told us, you weren't exactly happy with his landscaping services from what we found on his web site. Didn't you call him a cretin and—"

"Get the hell outta here." She screamed as she rose unsteadily to her feet. "I want both of you to hit the road. Now!"

"But, Ms. Ellis, I just have a few more questions."

Joe Earl elbowed me.

"I've asked you to leave." Liz pointed at the door, her face now twisted with rage. "If you don't go, I'll call the police. Or worse." She tossed a coaster at us. Joe Earl ducked.

Then, she lobbed another one at us.

"Hey, stop throwing stuff at us." He slipped his iPhone in the holster to protect it.

Liz snatched up a large pillow and hurled it in my direction. It missed, but knocked over a lamp.

"All right, we're leaving." I jumped up, grabbing Joe Earl's arm as our irate hostess aimed a ceramic ashtray at my head. Before she could throw it, or any other missiles, we ran for the foyer and hurried out of the house. I heard the ashtray hit the door with a thud behind us.

"That woman is a whacko," Joe Earl said as we jogged toward my truck.

"I shouldn't have pushed her so hard, especially after I smelled the gin," I admitted. "She probably downed half a bottle this morning."

"Maybe more."

"Let's hit the road. I'm getting a bad feeling about her." I cranked up the engine and reversed out of the driveway. As we started to pull away, I spied Liz on her front lawn, heaving a shovel at us. It narrowly missed Rusty's hood.

"Hit the gas," Joe Earl urged. Instantly, my foot rammed down the pedal, and the engine died. Panic spurted through me as I turned the key in the ignition and pumped the pedal.

"She's picking up a pair of hedge clippers!"

I heard them clunk inside my truck's bed.

Come on, start! Rusty's engine fired up, and we sped off. "What the hell is going on? That's the second time someone has attacked me today."

Joe Earl checked the side-view mirror. "I don't know. Bad karma?"

"Don't start sounding like Madame Geri. I just couldn't take it." I tried to rein in my rioting nerves. "Good thing she'd had a lot to drink 'cause her reflexes were slower. Otherwise, Rusty might be missing a taillight."

"You think? She was going for a chain saw when the clippers didn't cause more damage."

Shoving back my hair, I kept my hands on the wheel and my eyes fastened on the road. "Who would've thought someone could go *that* berserk just talking about Bucky McGuire?"

"She's going up to the top of the suspect list, that's for sure," Joe Earl said in a grim tone.

"I guess being on the verge of bankruptcy doesn't help." I turned onto the main drag leading back to the Coral Island and increased my speed. "We're going to have to tell Nick Billie what happened. She seemed crazy enough to murder anyone, including Bucky."

"You can say that again."

"Well, we're safe now, and we can swing by the police station later today."

All of a sudden, Rusty lurched forward with a jarring impact that caused our heads to snap forward. A sharp pain shot up the back of my neck. Then I checked my rearview mirror.

Holy hell.

Liz Ellis sat behind the wheel of a red Lincoln Town Car, her face transformed into a demonic grin as she mouthed, "I said that you'd be sorry. Damn you." Honking the horn in one long blast, she drew closer. And closer.

"Brace yourself!" I shouted. "She's trying to kill us!"

Chapter Thirteen

Joe Earl muttered an expletive and placed both hands on the dashboard, elbows straight, chin up, eyes fixed on the side mirror.

I fingered my seat belt to check for a snug fit, then gripped the steering wheel so tightly that my fingers turned numb. Not daring to move my glance off the road again, I couldn't gauge exactly where Liz was right now in her vehicular attack, but I tromped on the gas pedal.

"Can't you go any faster?" Joe Earl yelled out.

"I've got it floored."

Joe Earl leaned over to check the speedometer and snorted. "We're only doing fifty-five!"

"That's all Rusty's got! You'd better call 9-1-1."

He reached for his iPhone, but it slipped out of his hands. "Damn, it fell under the seat." Fumbling to retrieve it, he cursed under his breath. "I can't reach the cell unless I unhook my seat belt."

"Don't even think about it!" Frantically taking a quick peep in the rearview mirror again, I watched in horror as the massive car bore down on us. We'd cleared Paradisio, and the road had narrowed to a two-lane with mangroves on either side, clear sailing in terms of speed limit, and she was gaining on us with every second. "There's nowhere to pull off."

Joe Earl looked briefly over his shoulder. "Is she driving a tank or what?"

"Lincoln Town Car. They're designed to take out small cities." I eked out another five miles per hour, causing Rusty's steering wheel to shimmy like a drunken hula dancer. "We're no match for that beast of a car. A couple of hard bumps, and she could push us into the mangroves. I've got to do something."

"Any time, Mallie."

A wave of fear swept through me. "I'm going to try something crazy, but I've only seen it done on TV. I'm not sure it will work, but the Coral Island Water station is coming up, and it has a small driveway that we might—"

"Do it!"

I jerked the wheel to the left and yanked on the emergency brake. The back tires locked as I pumped the brakes lightly and steered in a wide arc, causing a piercing squeal and burning rubber. Rusty tipped to one side, but I held the wheel firm and let up on the e-brake. We hit the gravel and spun around. I screamed something that came out like, "Yaaaghhhh!" After a few seconds, the back of my truck hit a chain-link fence and came to an abrupt halt.

Panting, I kept my death grip on the wheel as I saw Liz's Town Car try to execute the same maneuver and fly into a shallow canal on the opposite side of the road. The square trunk of her Lincoln tipped upward like a ship's stern, but the vehicle didn't slide under. It remained upright, emergency lights blinking, back wheels still spinning.

"She d-didn't know the e-brake trick," I stammered, trying to calm my ragged breathing.

"Where did you learn to drive like that?" Joe Earl squeaked.

"I spent a lot of time watching the *Bourne* movies when I worked at Disneyworld. Lots of good chase scenes. They could be a primer on how to drive in an emergency. My favorite was the *Bourne Ultimatum.*" Okay, I was officially babbling, but I had an excuse. "I guess it's safe now to retrieve your cell phone and call 9-1-1."

He unbuckled his seat belt, reached under the seat for his iPhone, and tucked it firmly in the holster. "No way. She tried to rear-end us."

"I'll do it—" But another car had already stopped, the middle-aged driver jumping out and flipping open his cell phone with one fluid motion. "Hang on, I'm calling the police!" he shouted. "Honk if you can hear me."

Liz gave a loud blast.

"She's alive. Let's get out of here." I turned back onto Coral Island Road, driving very slowly and carefully. Reaction was setting in, and waves of post-traumatic stress washed over me, causing me to shake all over.

"You can kick it up to thirty."

"No, dammit," I said, trying to force myself to relax by chanting my mantra: "Muggatoni. Muggatoni. Muggatoni."

"Hey, I'm on *your* side," he retorted.

"Sorry." Abandoning the mantra, I realized that nothing would help calm me at this point. I'd almost been turned into roadkill twice in one day, and it wasn't even noon yet. My nerves were edgier than a razor blade cutting grass.

"Do you want me to call Nick Billie and tell him what happened?"

"Uh . . . eventually." I turned left at the island center's four-way stop. "I need to swing by the tilapia farm first and pick up some evidence from Pop Pop. I told him I'd get it this morning, but that was before a snake almost bit me, a monster truck tried to run me over, and Liz Ellis tried to rear-end us into that great dead motorists' heaven in the sky."

"I don't think we should wait too long to contact him. She's out of control."

"True, but it's going to take a little time to pull her car out of the canal. Just long enough for me to touch base with Pop Pop.

To be honest, I'm more than a little worried about him."

"Because of that Travis dude?"

"Not exactly. I didn't tell you this, but he's been trying to unionize the other oldie co-workers and has gone kind of over the top. Aunt Lily said he and his co-workers were hitting the tequila pretty hard last night at Le Sink."

"Seriously?"

"He answers his cell phone with 'United Tilapia Farmworkers Union,' and some guy from Tallahassee is coming today to help them do a vote."

"And you thought I was eccentric because I had a violin with the image of Old Abe?"

"Point taken."

We drove the rest of the way in silence. Once at the tilapia farm, I parked Rusty in the empty lot outside the main office, asking Joe Earl to stay in my truck, ready to text me if Travis appeared on the scene. After taking a quick scan of the grounds, I hurried toward the tent where the tilapia tanks were housed.

"Pop Pop?" I poked my head in the maintenance shed and scanned the interior for his familiar wrinkled face and oxygen tank, but he was nowhere to be seen. Tapping my toes, I speed dialed him. After several interminable rings, he picked up. "I'm at the tilapia farm. Where are you?" I hissed.

"Inside the tent. Behind the generator."

Sidling in that direction, I ducked inside and spotted Pop Pop coming toward me. Then I did a double take. He'd ditched his trademark plaid shorts and button-down shirt for a pair of camouflage overalls and Che Guevara hat, along with a UTFU button on his t-shirt. He'd also slapped a UNION NOW! sticker over his oxygen tank.

"Why did you take so long to answer?" I said, torn between relief and irritation.

"*Tranquilo, chica.* I'm on lunch break right now with Jose and

Pepe, so I don't have to answer the phone." He held up a half-eaten taco, the sauce dripping down his earth-toned t-shirt. "We're getting ready to count the votes now that they're in. Our organizer is really pleased with the turnout."

"There are only three of you working here."

He shook a gnarly fist and took a whiff of oxygen. "Power to the old people!"

"Listen, *hombre,* I've had a really, really tough day, and I'm not in the mood for any nonsense. Your main reason for being here is to scope out evidence against Travis," I remarked, spacing out the last three words for emphasis, "not organize two old guys who'll probably be going on strike at the retirement home."

"We'll see." A smug grin spread over his face. "Just 'cause you're the editor-boss now, you've forgotten the workers' plight."

Gritting my teeth, I counted to ten. "Pop Pop, I need that bleach bottle. Where is it?"

"Lemme see if my lunch break is over." Pop Pop checked his watch, squinting to make out the dial. "I'm still off the clock for another five minutes, but I'll count it toward my overtime. I hid the bottle in the tool cabinet over there, so our management oppressor wouldn't find it. Here, hold this." He handed me the soggy taco.

As he tottered off, I caught a delicious aroma of beef and salsa. My mouth watering, I realized that with all of the craziness today, I'd skipped my normal burger and fries midday snack. Keeping a wary eye on Pop Pop's retreating back, I took a nibble. The spicy sauce melted on my tongue in a delicious explosion of grease and meat.

"Go ahead and finish it off, Mallie," he said, without turning around as he rooted in the cabinet.

I didn't need to be told twice. In three chomps, I had gobbled down the rest of the taco and licked the last bit of sauce off my fingers. *Delicioso.*

As Pop Pop returned, the bleach bottle balanced on top of his oxygen tank, he cocked his head to one side with a triumphant expression. "Told you I'd get the goods on Travis."

"I never doubted you." Well, maybe a little.

"When we negotiate pay, I'm going to make sure that Pepe gets a little extra to make his lip-smacking taco lunches."

"He should patent the sauce." I gave my index finger another once over, then grabbed the bottle and refocused on the matter at hand, the tanks with hundreds of dead fish floating belly-up. At the very least, we had evidence that Travis was a fish killer. "Did you see Travis put this stuff in the water?"

Pop Pop held up his cell phone with a picture of Travis pouring bleach in the tilapia tank. "He was shaking that bottle like a *diablo* on a mission of death." His voice rose to a high pitch of outrage, causing him to cough and need another hit of oxygen.

"That's odd, because his business is going strong, financially speaking."

"He isn't just killing the fish; he grinds up the dead carcasses and puts them in his fertilizer." Pop Pop held up a canvas compost bag. "He's gone *loco.*"

Ohmigod. I cradled the bottle under my arm and placed the other one on his shoulder. "You need to come home to the Twin Palms; we need you there now that Wanda Sue has gone AWOL."

A slow smile spread across his face. "You're not fooling me, missy. You just want me back as your boyfriend, but I can't now. I've got bigger fish to fry."

I hoped he wasn't going to grill the bleach-bloated tilapia.

"Today the tilapia farm, tomorrow the palm-tree farms." He thumped his UTFU pin. "I intend to unionize every operation on Coral Island. Power to the people!"

As if on cue, Jose and Pepe hobbled in. They wore work jeans and t-shirts, but also sported UTFU buttons. Once they reached us, they began shouting, "Union! Union! Union!" Jose tapped his cane in time with the chant.

So much for being unobtrusive.

"Pop Pop, let me know how all that turns out. I'll get this evidence to Nick Billie." But my words fell on union-deafened ears. They were already marching out of the tent, chanting and wheezing all the way.

I took one last look at the dead tilapia and shuddered once more. Travis needed to be stopped, at least in terms of the contaminated fertilizer and animal abuse. Whether he or Liz killed Bucky remained to be seen.

Hotfooting it back to my truck, I slid in and handed the bleach bottle to Joe Earl. He was just wrapping up a conversation on his iPhone. "Okay, we'll be there in a few minutes."

"First thing, we have to drop this evidence off at the police station. It implicates Travis in poisoning his fish tanks. Pop Pop even snapped a picture of him doing it," I began, shifting Rusty into gear. "Then, we can also tell Nick what happened today with Liz Ellis's road rage."

"No can do. Your Aunt Lily just called and said we need to get back to the Twin Palms immediately. She said it was urgent and do not pass go. What does that mean?"

"It means tighten your seat belt. We've got to roll." I made a wild guess that Monopoly wasn't an iPhone app.

I hit the gas.

Fifteen minutes later, we breezed into the Twin Palms main office and found Aunt Lily standing behind the check-in counter, her head bent over the reservations book with a pencil tucked behind her ear.

"What's so urgent?" I asked.

She flipped the pages slowly. "You know, Wanda Sue's bookkeeping system really needs to be computerized. It's amazing that she makes any money at all."

"That's the emergency?"

"No." Aunt Lily snapped the book shut and finally looked up. "But it's part of it."

Joe Earl leaned against the counter. "TMAI."

"Tell me about it," I translated for her. "He's into texting big-time."

"LOL to you, too." Aunt Lily's mouth twisted wryly. "After I checked in a few newcomers this morning, I was going through Wanda Sue's reservations cabinet, and found this form, which I guess she misfiled." Aunt Lily produced a contract with the Shoreline Bank header. "It looks like Wanda Sue applied for a twenty-thousand-dollar loan on September twenty-sixth of this year for landscaping improvements to the Twin Palms RV sites. With the park as collateral. It was processed by Destiny Ransford, but the initials in the corner are TH."

My eyes widened as her words sank in. "Travis Harper."

"Could he sign off on a loan that big?" Joe Earl chimed in.

"Sure. The park is worth way more than that." Aunt Lily flipped over the loan form to reveal a scrap of lined paper from a yellow legal pad. "Here's the interesting part. Clipped to the loan paper was Wanda Sue's handwritten note to cancel her application because she decided not to buy expensive greenery from Liz Ellis's nursery."

My breath caught in my throat. "When did she change her mind?"

"Three days ago. Right before that infamous town-council meeting." She paused, pointing at some nearly illegible sentences scrawled at the bottom of the page. "Wanda Sue claimed the nursery plants weren't up to par."

"Because of Bucky's contaminated fertilizer," I interjected, my thoughts racing faster than an eight-cylinder Mustang. "Travis was putting bleach-bloated tilapia in Bucky's fertilizer, not to sabotage *his* business, but to bankrupt Bucky's landscaping business, and maybe ruin his clients, too. I'm curious who signed off on Liz Ellis's loan."

"Bucky must've found out about the fertilizer and asked Travis to meet him after the town-hall meeting. They argued, fought, then Travis whapped Bucky on the back of the head with the frying pan to implicate Wanda Sue."

"That means Travis must've planned it," Aunt Lily pointed out.

"You both rock." Joe Earl high-fived me and my aunt.

"But why did he want to take over Bucky's and Liz's businesses?" Aunt Lily's brows knit in bafflement. "They were small potatoes."

"They add up. I'm sure he wanted to add their companies to his little island empire," Joe Earl said. "From what I see in his financial statements, he was becoming a wealthy man bit by bit."

"We need definite proof." My elation dimmed like a flickering bulb of indecision for a few seconds. Then it surged brightly again as a thought occurred to me. "Destiny Ransford can tell us for sure."

"Mallie, you'd better call Nick Billie first." Aunt Lilly picked up the office phone and handed it to me.

"It's just a theory. I don't have any proof." I replaced the receiver.

She gave me a hard stare.

"All right, I'll call him on my way to the bank, and I'll take Joe Earl with me. Safe enough?"

Her glance didn't waver. "I don't like it."

But we were already out the door.

"So you don't think Liz Ellis did it?" Joe Earl opened Rusty's passenger door. "Even after she tried to mow us down with her mega-car?"

"Not after hearing this evidence. Liz is probably just an angry ex who had a major meltdown and, unfortunately, we took the brunt of it." Back at the wheel again, I cranked up Rusty's engine and drove off.

On the way, I called Nick to tell him that we were following up a lead, but his phone went straight to voice mail. *Rats.* I left him a message that didn't seem too rambling to me, but Joe Earl kept making a slicing motion across his neck to wrap it up. I put my motor mouth in neutral.

Then, I speed dialed Madame Geri, who picked up on the first ring. "We're heading to Shoreline Bank to question Destiny."

"Be careful," she warned. "The violin started vibrating again."

"Will do."

As we pulled up in front of the bank, I noticed the parking lot was empty, and fallen palm fronds covered the crushed-shell walkway. "It looks deserted."

"Island hours." Joe Earl followed my glance. "Everybody leaves at noon on Friday."

I sighed. "Anita never lets us knock off early."

"You could change that."

"Fat chance. I'm just warming her seat until she gets back." Still, I had made the deadline for this week's edition of the *Observer* with only a phony psychic and an iPhone-a-holic sidekick to help out. *Not bad.* I clicked off the engine with a decisive snap. Maybe I could fill in for Anita again. Just not too soon.

We exited Rusty.

Once we reached the entrance, Joe Earl tugged on the glass door's handle. It swung open. I gave him a thumbs-up and we entered the lobby.

"What are you doing here?" Destiny demanded as she strolled out of her office. Her face still looked blotchy from crying. Hair pulled back tightly, she wore brown, linen dress pants and a matching jacket, buttoned up and smoothly pressed. "We've closed for the day."

"If I could just have a few minutes of your time; I need to ask you a couple of questions."

She folded her arms across her chest and started tapping the toe of her high-heeled shoe. "I'm very busy."

"This won't take long." I fished around in my hobo bag and pulled out my notebook. Flipping through the pages, I scanned my scrawls until I found her interview remarks. "Didn't you say that you had been . . . involved romantically with Bucky?"

Her eyes teared up and her mouth trembled.

"Was there anyone else in your life at the time?" I probed.

"No." Destiny spat it out quickly. Too quickly.

"The investigation into Bucky's death is still open, but something else did turn up that I wanted to ask you about. It seems that Wanda Sue applied for a big loan here at Shoreline Bank, and you approved it."

A shadow of wariness flashed across her face. "Yes, that's true. I review all loan applications."

"And Travis Harper approves them, as well?" I asked quietly, watching her reaction. "He's on the board of directors, I believe."

The toe tapping halted abruptly, and her arms dropped to her sides. "I . . . I think you'd better leave," she said in a small voice, her eyes darting around the room.

"We're not going anywhere." Joe Earl moved closer until he stood next to me.

"I have nothing else to say," she managed to get out.

"Is it true? Was Travis approving bad loans?" I hammered at her.

Her hands picked at her jacket hem. "Maybe. I don't know. You need to leave *now.*"

"Was the bad blood between Travis and Bucky on account of you? Did Travis want you for himself?"

"Absolutely not! Travis was old enough to be my father." Her outrage at least seemed genuine.

"Then what was it?" Joe Earl queried.

She buried her face in her hands and mumbled, "I told Bucky about the loans."

Excitement lurched inside of me. "And that Travis had you doing his illegal, dirty deals."

"They were legitimate, at first," she explained, raising her head with a loud exhalation. "Some of the small businesses defaulted, and Travis bought them up. Then he started pushing me to approve bigger and bigger loans to companies that had no hope of paying them back." Her eyes turned pleading. "I didn't want to do it, but Travis found out that I'd taken a few thousand for myself when he reviewed the annual audit."

"You were embezzling?" Disbelief threaded through my voice. I was definitely *not* opening an account in this bank.

"I had medical bills from when my mother was dying," she confessed. "Honestly, I was going to pay it all back, turn Travis in, and take my punishment, all because of Bucky. He made me want to tell the truth about everything."

"Except about his murder," I said.

"I was too afraid of Travis, and I knew they'd never arrest Wanda Sue."

My head was spinning at the web of lies, and the noble portrait of Bucky. "Let me get this straight: Travis blackmailed you into processing the loans, you told Bucky, and he confronted Travis."

"Not at first. I wanted to pay back the money I'd taken, so I asked Bucky to wait. But Travis got suspicious when I slowed down processing any more loans. Liz Ellis's second mortgage was the last one." She bit her lip and tears rolled down her cheeks. "At that point, we realized that Travis was putting something in Bucky's fertilizer to ruin his business. We had to stop him."

"And it all erupted at the town hall," I finished for her.

She nodded. "Bucky and I argued before the meeting about when to confront Travis. Afterwards, they met and Bucky told Travis that he was going to the authorities . . ." she faltered.

"But he wouldn't accept it," I prompted.

"That's why I had to kill him," Travis explained as he appeared at her side.

He held a gun in his right hand.

Chapter Fourteen

"I *told* you to leave." Destiny said to Joe Earl and me, wringing her hands. "He arrived right before you did and was listening to everything we said from my office."

"Dirtbag," Joe Earl said.

"Sticks and stones." Travis wagged a finger back and forth with a tsk-tsk sound. "There's no need to be rude, my boy."

"Oh, please, drop the southern-gentleman routine. We all know what you are now: a slimy killer," I said, throwing caution to the winds. "Nick Billie is on his way here right now, so you might as well put the weapon down. It's over."

"Not quite." He checked his watch. "If I'm not mistaken, at this very minute, Nick is heading to Cresswell's Retro Diner on a hot tip that Wanda Sue may be hiding out there."

Fear swept through me as I eyed the distance to the front door. *Damn.* Too far away.

Travis moved next to Destiny and slipped an arm across her shoulders, but he kept his razor-sharp eyes on me. "I could tell that you were closing in on the truth about the loans. So I figured it was time to dispose of Destiny but, before I had the chance, you showed up. So I get a two-fer . . . or, rather, a three-fer. This isn't as carefully planned out as the frying-pan attack on Bucky, but sometimes you have to improvise."

"No, please," Destiny whimpered.

"Don't worry. You won't feel a thing when I put a bullet right here." He kissed her forehead, and she visibly shuddered. "We had a good thing going, Destiny. Until you grew a conscience. Too bad."

"It won't take long for Nick to figure out what happened," I warned, puffing out my thin chest with bravado that I was far from feeling. "A lot of people know we were on our way here. Aunt Lily and the entire staff at the *Observer.*" I hoped he couldn't hear my knees knocking.

"I'll be gone by then with the money from the last loan that I just approved, for two million dollars against my own company." He remained calm. "More improvising after Bucky tried to stop my expanding financial enterprise."

"So, you decided not just to destroy Bucky's business, but close down yours as well?" My question was more of a statement.

"Only recently. Since he started sniffing around my banking activities." Travis smiled. "Then, after our little fracas at the town-council meeting, I realized that I'd have to eliminate him altogether and liquidate my assets. Sad, but necessary." He flexed his fingers around the gun. "I have to give you credit, Snoop Girl. In spite of the messy clothes, rat's-nest hair, and bumbling investigation, you've got some grit, I'll give you that. I put that rattlesnake in your truck and tried to run you over afterwards. And still you survived—and kept digging. Not bad."

"Bastard!" Joe Earl spat at his shoes.

Travis jerked back his foot, giving Joe Earl a much-needed nanosecond to whip out his iPhone and snap a picture.

"What the hell are you doing?" Travis yelled out. "Give me that damn cell phone!"

"Too late," Joe Earl said, holding it up with a wide grin. "I already posted your picture on Facebook, so the whole world can see you holding the gun on us."

"Welcome to the world of digital natives," I sang out, still smarting over the rat's-nest hair comment.

Travis roared a string of vicious insults at us, knocking the iPhone out of Joe Earl's hand. It crashed to the ground but didn't break. It just bounced, snapping pictures with every clunk on the floor.

Destiny elbowed Travis in the side and ran for the door, her arms and legs pumping hard. But she barely covered a few feet before he squeezed off a shot that grazed her leg. She screamed and went down, with a dark red stain streaked across her calf. She curled into the fetal position, rocking and sobbing.

"Looks like I'm going to Plan B: kill everyone and take my chances." Laughing wildly, he aimed the gun at her again. "I've already got my ticket booked to Costa Rica, and I just might get there before they find your bodies."

"No!" I yelled, lunging at him. But I tripped on the carpet and fell to my knees, the contents of my hobo bag—checkbook, pen, lipstick, and stapler—spilling out over the floor.

"Ditz," he mocked, leveling the gun at Destiny again. I grabbed for the stapler and rammed a few staples into his ankle. He yelped and kicked me in the side. I winced in pain, feeling my rib crack. Joe Earl then barreled into him and they went down.

At that moment the front door swung open. *Nick?* I looked up and blinked in disbelief.

Not Nick.

Pop Pop stood there, haloed in the afternoon light, wearing full camouflage gear with the oxygen tank at his side. Jose and Pepe stood behind him in similar outfits, waving yellow, plastic baseball bats and shouting in Spanish.

"Get him, brothers!" Pop Pop took a whiff of oxygen and motioned his cohorts forward. *"Andale!"*

Jose and Pepe swarmed around Travis, beating him with the plastic bats, while Pop Pop butted him with the wheels of his oxygen tank, shouting, "We're kicking ass for the working class!"

Joe Earl quickly rolled out of the way.

I grabbed Travis's gun and stood up, reaching for my cell phone to call 9-1-1. But before I could punch in the numbers, Nick Billie came jogging through the door, followed by Deputy Brad. His glance moved from Destiny on the floor, to the seniors wielding their bats, to me holding the gun.

"It wasn't my fault," I began.

"Later." Nick waded into the melee, brushing aside the geezer squad and cuffing Travis. "Phone for an ambulance," he instructed his deputy, who knelt next to Destiny and immediately made the call.

Yanking Travis to his feet, Nick kept a tight grasp on his arm. Disheveled and breathing heavily, Travis swayed back and forth on unsteady legs, glaring at his attackers.

Pepe and Jose held out their bats in a defensive posture.

Nick turned to me. "I'm not even going to ask why Pop Pop and his friends are beating Travis with plastic bats."

Pop Pop pointed at his union button. "We just formed Local 3218 of the United Tilapia Farmworkers Union today and wanted to take down our oppressor."

"He was undercover at the tilapia farm," I admitted, then averted my glance. "And then he . . . just showed up with Pepe and Jose."

"We followed him 'cause we knew he was up to no good when he emptied out all the cash from the office," Pop Pop explained.

"Si," his buddies joined in.

Clearing my throat, I continued, "It was Travis all along."

"He killed Bucky," Destiny moaned in a weak voice.

"I know." Nick's mouth tightened into a grim line. "I was building my case right after Wanda Sue's frying pan turned up outside the town hall. She'd told me last year that she left it at Bucky's house after she tried to attack him. So I knew the killer had probably stolen the pan out of Bucky's house, then attacked him with it and tried to frame Wanda Sue."

"Fingerprints?" I asked.

"Fish residue."

Joe Earl gagged.

"The fish were full of the same bleach as the tilapia near Bucky's body and the fish at Travis's farm."

"You knew about the bleach?" I clutched my broken rib.

A wry but indulgent glint appeared in his eyes. "You sent Liz Ellis to me, and I investigated her complaint."

"She tried to run us down with her car," I sputtered.

"Smart woman," Travis said.

Nick inclined his head at the sentiment. "I figured that Travis had replenished the town-hall tank, carrying them in the frying pan, with fish from his farm. But he put white tilapia in the tank, not red ones. He's the only person on the island who farms white tilapia." Nick glanced over at Destiny, who was lying still as the deputy held pressure on her leg. "I knew it had something to do with you since you were the link between the two of them, and I'd been following Travis's financial dealings at the bank for some time. A lot of small business owners had complained about him."

She closed her eyes and nodded.

"Travis was blackmailing her into approving bad loans to bankrupt companies that he wanted to buy up cheap," I supplied, grimacing every time I took in a breath. "Bucky wanted her to confess—"

"Save it," Nick cut in. "Everyone is going to have to come to the police station and give a full statement."

I heard sirens approaching. "Maybe you could go easy on me, Nick. I may have a broken rib."

"She's trouble," Travis said.

"Don't I know it?" Nick escorted him out, flashing me an

"I'll-deal-with-you-later" look.

Mea culpa.

Epilogue

"It's good to be home again at the Twin Palms, and I sure do appreciate all of you risking your lives for me so I wouldn't be tossed in the clink." Wanda Sue glanced around the picnic table next to my Airstream, bestowing a smile on Joe Earl, Madame Geri, and Bernice, who were munching on a large plate of stone-crab claws with various dips. "And I'm pleased as punch that I've been appointed to the town council without even an election."

Bernice propped her arm and wrist casts on the table top, dipping her claw into melted butter. "All the other candidates are in jail or dead."

"That's not true," Wanda Sue protested, then she pursed her mouth. "Well, I guess it is. But I would've won the election anyway."

"You bet." I cracked a claw and dipped the meaty part into mustard sauce. "But your new political career is going to take you away from managing the RV park. Is Pop Pop going to be able to pick up the slack now he's become a union organizer?" I hadn't seen him since the plastic-bat attack, but I kept getting *Union Now!* literature on my truck windshield.

"Not to worry, honey. I've got it under control." She patted my hand. "I hired Coop as Pop Pop's new assistant. I think he'll work out just fine as long as he can remember what he needs to do."

Oh, boy.

I pulled my sweater tighter around my taped ribs, trying not to take in a breath too deeply; it still hurt. A cool breeze was drifting in off the Gulf as the sun was setting in Mango Bay, lighting the sky in streaks of yellow and orange. *Happy colors.* "I'm just relieved that Travis will be put away for a long, long time. And I don't have to worry about snakes in my truck anymore."

"Me, too." Joe Earl popped a piece of crab in his mouth.

"I also heard from Nick that Destiny will probably get a reduced sentence for embezzlement because she's agreed to testify against Travis," I added. "All good news."

"So our island cop isn't mad at you?" Wanda Sue asked with a tiny grin.

"We've declared a truce." I glanced over at the empty site where Cole had parked his van, then down at my right hand where I'd removed the engagement ring. My decision had been made. Detective Billie was the man for me.

I'd miss Cole. He'd been part of my life at a time when I didn't know what I wanted or if I'd ever find it once I knew. But that was the past. We'd parted as friends the day he left, and I'd be lying if I said I didn't feel a tiny pang of loss inside. No regrets, though.

Anita would be back in a day or two, and I could have some extra time to settle into a new relationship with Nick.

Life was really looking up.

"Let's not forget to thank the spirit world. They were advising us all along through the Abe Lincoln violin." Madame Geri produced the battered old instrument and set it next to the crab-claw platter. "It pointed us to the bridal magazine cover with the pond, a symbol of the fish tanks at Travis's tilapia farm. We just couldn't figure it out at the time. Also, it warned us that Mallie was in danger."

The violin started to vibrate wildly, and we all sat back.

"Old Abe is riled up again," Wanda Sue exclaimed. "Maybe it's a new prediction."

Madame Geri placed her fingertips on the violin and closed her eyes briefly. Then she shrugged. "A big surprise is coming. That's all I'm getting."

Exhaling with impatience, I picked up the violin and shook it. Something clunked. Turning it upside down, I caught Marley the Parrot's pet pager as it dropped out.

"He must've dropped it in there during Bernice's first bicycle accident." Madame Geri took it from me and slipped it into her purse. "Silly bird."

"That's why the stupid violin was vibrating." Bernice gave an exclamation of disgust.

"A coincidence," Joe Earl said.

Just then, a Toyota Camry pulled up and parked in front of my Airstream. Moments later, a young guy with a crew cut and suit strolled over. "Which of you is Mallie Monroe?"

I raised my hand.

He set a folded piece of paper on my table. "Ms. Liz Ellis is suing you for defamation of character, intent to do her bodily harm with your vehicle, and theft of a pair of hedge clippers."

"What?" I sat back in shock. "She's the one who tried to run *me* over. And she threw those clippers at us."

"I can't comment. I'm just a legal assistant in her attorney's office." He gave a little salute. "Have a nice day."

After he drove off, I tore the paper in half. "That's what I think of this big surprise. Can you believe the gall of that crazy woman?" *So much for my happy colors.*

"Don't worry, Mallie, you've got friends in high places—me and Nick Billie." Wanda Sue thumped her chest in pride. "We'll protect you."

Ah, yes . . . Nick.

As relief spread through me, the lyrics of Beyonce's "Crazy in

Love" blasted out from my neighbor's fifth-wheeler RV. It was the type of melody for . . . newlyweds.

Aha!

It wasn't a famous singer parked next door, but a person who liked famous love songs.

Instantly, I rose to my feet and slid out from the table's seat, careful not to jar my ribs. "I know who's over there. It's Anita and Benton in an RV rental from Miami, and she's probably been spying on us like she did once before." I marched over to the RV and banged on the door. "Come on out, you honeymooners. Right now!"

An exotic, dark-haired woman appeared, wearing a cream-colored sweater and matching silk pants.

Not Anita by a long shot.

"Oh, sorry." I offered an apologetic smile. "I thought you were someone else."

"Hi, I'm Ramira Billie. Nick's wife."

My smile froze.

ABOUT THE AUTHOR

Marty Ambrose is a multi-published mystery author. At present, she is living the dream on an island in southwest Florida, dividing her time between writing and teaching English at a local state college.

Marty began her writing career in romantic suspense and published two novels with Avalon Books and, later, three novels for Kensington. She then moved into her real love, stemming from the time that she first read Agatha Christie's Miss Marple books: cozy mysteries. She published four books featuring her quirky amateur sleuth, Mallie Monroe, in the successful Mango Bay Mystery series with Thomas & Mercer; *Coastal Corpse* is the fifth in the series.

And so the dream continues . . .